"I am going ... alone…"

"Our baby," Jame... her throat constri... possession in his...

"I don't need your help in this, James."

"It's not about what *you* need. It's about what the baby needs," James said. "Though I'd suggest that you do need some help. I've heard on the grapevine that your credit card has been stopped… I guess Mommy and Daddy are not very amused with their daughter's behavior."

"I doubt that they will ever speak with me again," Leila said, "so I doubt I will find out."

James looked at her and felt a bit bad then— his parents were trouble enough but Leila was dealing with a king and queen. "I'm sure they'll come around."

He took a breath. A gnaw of disquiet was growing as the ramifications of that thought hit home. Yes, her parents would surely come around and what then?

What happened then to the princess and her baby?

What happened to *his* child?

"How did your parents take the news?" Leila asked.

"I'm not here to talk about our families," James said. "I'm here to sort things out between us."

The world's most elite hotel is looking for a jewel in its crown and Spencer Chatsfield has found it. But Isabella Harrington, the girl from his past, refuses to sell!

Now the world's most decadent destinations have become a chessboard in this game of power, passion and pleasure...

Welcome to

The Chatsfield

Synonymous with style, sensation...and scandal!

With the eight Chatsfield siblings happily married and settling down, it's time for a new generation of Chatsfields to shine!

Spencer Chatsfield steps in as CEO, determined to prove his worth. But when he approaches Isabella Harrington, of Harringtons Boutique Hotels, with the offer of a merger that would benefit them both...he's left with a stinging red palm-shaped mark on his cheek!

And so begins a game of cat and mouse that will shape the future of the Chatsfields and the Harringtons forever.

But neither knows that there's one stakeholder with the power to decide their fate...and their identity will shock both the Harringtons *and* the Chatsfields.

Just who will come out on top?

Find out in

Eight titles to collect—you won't want to miss out!

Princess's Secret Baby

Carol Marinelli

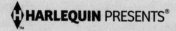

HARLEQUIN PRESENTS®

ISBN-13: 978-0-373-13796-1

Princess's Secret Baby

First North American publication 2015

Copyright © 2015 by Harlequin Books S.A.

Special thanks and acknowledgment are given to Carol Marinelli for her contribution to The Chatsfield series.

Recycling programs
for this product may
not exist in your area.

HARLEQUIN®

www.Harlequin.com

Printed in U.S.A.

Carol Marinelli is a Taurus, with Taurus rising, yet still thinks she is a secret Gemini. Originally from England, she now lives in Australia and is a single mother of three. Apart from her children, writing romance and the friendships forged along the way are her passion. She chooses to believe in a happy-ever-after for all and strives for that in her writing.

Books by Carol Marinelli

Harlequin Presents

The Playboy of Puerto Banus
Playing the Dutiful Wife
Heart of the Desert
Innocent Secretary...Accidentally Pregnant

Alpha Heroes Meet Their Match
The Only Woman to Defy Him
More Precious than a Crown
Protecting the Desert Princess

Empire of the Sands
Banished to the Harem
Beholden to the Throne

The Secrets of Xanos
A Shameful Consequence
An Indecent Proposition

Visit the author profile page
at Harlequin.com for more titles

CHAPTER ONE

'I WISH THAT it had been you!'

Princess Leila Al-Ahmar of Surhaadi froze as finally Queen Farrah voiced her truth.

Deep down Leila had always known that her mother would have preferred for it to be Leila, rather than her sister, Jasmine, who had died on that terrible night. Having it verified though, hearing her mother say the words that no parent ever should, felt like an arrow was right now being shot through Leila's heart and caused an agony that even she hadn't properly anticipated.

Not that Leila showed it to the woman who was now staring her down.

Only at night, only in sleep, did Leila cry for a love she had never been shown.

The absence of love in her life had made Leila resilient though, so she stood, unflinching, as her mother poured boiling oil onto already raw wounds. Only it wasn't just resilience that made Leila stand proud and silent—quite simply she was too stunned to react.

For all of her twenty-four years Leila had done everything she could to avoid this moment, but she had finally stopped running from the truth tonight.

After dinner, instead of heading to her suite, instead of disappearing, Leila had taken up her beloved *qanun*—a small harp that was so much more than an instrument to Leila. It was both her friend and her companion. It was gentle and pure and wild at times too, and when she played it Leila knew for sure that love existed.

Even if she had never known it from her parents.

Farrah loathed that her daughter adored music so.

Jasmine had played better apparently, Farrah said as she took up her embroidery. It was the same tapestry that she had been working on for more than sixteen years.

Night after night she unpicked the threads and resewed, going over and over it and refusing to finish as Leila's father sat silent in the chair.

No, she hadn't played better than me, Leila wanted to scream, for she knew that was not true.

Jasmine, her mother goaded, had held a note until doves lined the palace windows just to hear her play.

Tension had been building for years, yet on this night Leila had refused to give in and obey her mother's silent command to remove herself. Instead she had continued to play— plucking the *qanun*'s strings, refusing to be quiet, as was the unspoken rule in the palace.

Had her older brother, Zayn, been here he would have, by now, defused the situation. Zayn would have diverted their mother somehow.

But Zayn wasn't here tonight.

Soon he would marry the woman whom he had been betrothed to since childhood, Leila thought.

Even though she was twenty-four Leila's marriage had not yet been arranged—it upset her mother too much to get around to it, for Jasmine would have been such a beautiful bride, Jasmine would have had such adorable babies.

Jasmine, Jasmine, Jasmine.

She would be a spinster forever, Leila thought. She would be here alone in this palace with them until the day that she died.

Night after night spent hiding in her suite would be her life and so she brought things to a head tonight in the only way she knew how.

Leila said with her fingers, with each pluck of the strings, what could not be voiced by her mouth.

They told the truth.

The harmony that she created was not a peaceful one.

It spoke of the night sixteen years ago when Jasmine had died.

Leila had been only eight at the time but she remembered it well and, as an adult, she understood more clearly what had happened.

The music she made spoke of a young woman going off the rails. It spoke of drugs and drink and hips that had provocatively swayed as she'd danced with Zayn's best friend at that time. The music spoke of things that, even now, Leila didn't properly understand for she was, and had always tried to be, a good girl. Yet tonight her fingers spoke of sex and forbidden fruits and a young girl taking a dance with the devil himself.

'Leila…' Her mother spat. 'Enough!'

But still Leila's fingers strummed on.

Deep into her music she went. Exploring Zayn's fury and anger when he had found out how his friend had betrayed him with his sister.

Leila recalled some of the furious words that had poured from her brother, things that even now Leila could not really comprehend—how men like Jasmine's lover used women, that it was only the thrill of the chase that had them keen. How, now that he had had her, soon he would not want her.

Zayn had thrown Jasmine's lover out into the night and Jasmine had made the decision to follow him. Their mother, to this day, had Zayn almost eaten alive with guilt over the repercussions.

Leila's fingers revealed the screams that had filled the palace when the terrible news had hit that a car accident had left the young princess and her lover dead.

With not a word uttered, Leila exposed the truth of that night, with her musical talent.

'Khalas!' Her mother stood and screamed for her daughter to stop; she screamed for salvation. Farrah grabbed at the harp and sent it clattering to the floor, and as Leila's stood to retrieve her most beloved possession, it was then that her mother said it—'I wish that it had been you!'

Leila's golden eyes met the furious gaze of her mother's, willing her to retract, silently begging Farrah to break down and take back what she had just said, but instead her mother clarified her words past the point of no return.

'I wish it had been you who died that night, Leila.'

Now Leila drew in a breath, now she fought back.

'You fail to surprise me, for you have wished me dead from the moment that I was born.' Leila's voice did not waver nor did it betray the agony of the truth behind each word that she spoke. 'You have never wanted me. Even as I nursed at your breast your milk tasted sour from your resentment.' Leila knew that might sound an illogical statement, but as far back as she could remember Leila had known that she wasn't wanted.

'It was the maids who fed you,' her mother, blameless to the last, said. 'It must have been one of their milk that was sour with resentment. They always complained you were such a greedy baby.'

Leila wished there was no gravity; she just wanted to leave the earth, to be lifted to space, to disappear.

Yet her feet stayed on the ground.

As she somehow must.

'Sadly for you, Mother, I didn't die that night. I'm alive. I *have* a life and I have already wasted far too much of it trying to win your love. Well, no more.'

Her mother said nothing and Leila turned on her heel and walked past her father, who sat with his head in his hands. It hurt that he had done nothing to intervene. Yes, Leila understood that his brain was still addled with grief even all these years after Jasmine's death, but his silence in this argument spoke volumes.

Her jewelled slippers made no sound on the marble floor as Leila swiftly walked and there was a notable absence of her mother's footsteps running behind her.

Hurt heaped on top of hurt as her mother

made no attempt to follow her youngest daughter and try to take back those cruel words. Leila wanted her mother to tell her that she was mistaken, that she was loved.

Leila passed the family portraits in the long hallway as she made her way to her suite. Always she walked quickly at this point, always she did her best not to look at the paintings that hurt so very much, but surely nothing more could hurt her now.

Leila slowed down and came to a halt and turned.

There on the walls of the palace was her history. There, for all to see, was the truth that Leila had always known and tonight had been cruelly confirmed.

The first painting that she examined was a large family portrait. Her parents were sitting in far happier times; her mother was holding Zayn and smiling as she gazed at the baby who would one day be king.

Leila adored her older brother. Zayn loathed injustice and had stepped in over and over for Leila. Growing up he had done all he could to shield her, and his protectiveness towards his youngest sister had only increased since Jasmine's death.

Her mother blamed Zayn for what had happened to Jasmine too.

He carried not just the grief of losing his sister, whom he had been closer in age with than Leila, but he carried the blame for her death. Leila's heart broke for him too.

Did she wish that Zayn was here tonight though?

No.

For there was nothing that Zayn could do to protect her from this.

He could not force their mother to love.

Leila's eyes moved to the next portrait and there was Jasmine—wearing her famous cheeky smile that her mother so often spoke about.

It wasn't a cheeky smile, Leila thought with a shiver; it was manipulative, for she had been on the receiving end of it often.

Jasmine has been everything that Leila wasn't. Jasmine was pretty and funny and charming too.

Leila was serious and diligent—and as she looked at a portrait that had all three children in it, Leila's heart ached for that child with confusion in her eyes.

Leila's hair was cut short and, unlike Jasmine, she had been chubby and plain, but far more unforgivable than that she had been born a girl.

A long and difficult birth had assured that there would be no more babies for the queen. Oh, how Leila had tried to be everything that her parents wanted—she had tried so hard to be as brave and fearless as Zayn and had begged to go out hunting with their father, only to have the queen mock her.

Leila stood there remembering the morning that she had taken scissors from the palace kitchen and smuggled them up to her bathroom. She had cut her long black hair, hoping that if she looked like a boy, then maybe she would be loved.

'You were *such* a good girl,' Leila said to the image, recalling her tears when her mother had found her in the bathroom with her hair beside her on the floor and how badly she had been spanked and shamed.

Her hair had grown back, the puppy fat had long since faded and a serious beauty had emerged.

Unnoticed.

Rather than cry, she walked to her suite.

'Dismissed,' she said to the maid who sat

outside but did not move to Leila's command, and so she reiterated. 'You are dismissed for the night.'

'But you might need me.'

'I don't *need* anyone,' Leila said. She knew the maids thought her arrogant—her mother did too—but arrogance was her shield and she wore it well now.

'Dismissed!' Leila hissed, and she waited till the confused woman had left before going into her suite.

Leila headed straight for her dressing room. It was filled with the most exquisite robes that had been handmade by the skilled palace seamstresses, then beaded and embroidered by Surhaadi women. It was not the gowns that held her interest though. Leila dropped to her knees and crawled behind them, reaching into the dark corner and dragging out a huge jewelled chest.

She found the key that was hidden in the pocket of one of her robes, but as she knelt to open the chest, Leila's hands were shaking and it was as if Jasmine was here with her again, for she could hear her voice.

'You have to hide these things for me. If

anybody found them I would get into so much trouble.'

'But what if they find them in my room?' Leila had asked.

'As if they would ever think to look through your things.' Jasmine had laughed at the very thought. 'The only thing that they'd expect to find are books and more books. Just hide these for me, Leila, please.'

'No.'

Jasmine had smiled that smile and given Leila a small cuddle, a little bit of contact that Leila craved. 'Please, Leila, do it for me?'

Leila had agreed.

Here was the proof that Jasmine had been far from perfect, Leila thought as she opened the trunk that had stayed locked for years. She wanted to run back to her parents, to hold the contraband up at them, to tell them once and for all that their memory of Jasmine was wrong.

Jasmine wasn't, nor ever had been, perfect. Even Zayn, who carried so much guilt over the death of his younger sister, didn't know the full extent of Jasmine's wild ways.

Yes, she had been far from perfect, Leila thought, looking at a short black dress that was scooped low at the front. There were high black heeled shoes too amongst other things and Leila examined them all now. She opened a bottle of vodka and sniffed it.

She would tell her parents; she would show them. Yet, even now, Leila knew that she couldn't do that to her sister.

Even when she had died, still Leila had played her part in protecting Jasmine's reputation—a day after the funeral a package from overseas had arrived at the palace addressed to Jasmine and Leila had smuggled it back up to her suite and had thrown it in the trunk unopened.

She picked up the package and Leila's slender fingers tore at the paper, wondering what might be inside. There was a small cellophane packet and she pulled out the contents. There was a velvet bra in the deepest red and as she opened it up a tiny pair of panties fell out. Leila ran the soft fabric through her fingers. It was decadent, it was provocative and it was sexy. It was everything that a young princess should not be.

It was, Leila thought, terribly beautiful too.

Leila picked up a packet of tablets and though naive and innocent, she knew it was the pill. She knew that if you took it each day you could have sex without consequence.

Leila tossed the packet back in the trunk and took out a lipstick. She read the label—Pride. What an inappropriate name, Leila thought as she opened it and saw that it was the same deep red as the underwear.

It should be called Shame.

But why?

It was she, Leila, who lived a life of shame.

Jasmine, even if her life had been cut short, had known fun. She had at least had her parents' love and must have known the bliss of being held in another's arms.

Her eyes were drawn again to the pills and Leila picked up the packet and punched one out.

Sin lay in the palm of her hand.

Oh, to be held by another, for even a moment.

Imagine how it must feel to be kissed?

Leila lowered her head, her tongue taking up the pill, and she swallowed it down.

She took out a small case that she used when travelling for official engagements. Her maids took care of her luggage but this was the one she would take on the royal plane.

Leila had a credit card—she used it to purchase books and music sheets online.

Could she use it to purchase a flight?

She was running away, Leila realised as she went in her dresser and took out her passport.

But to where?

Leila picked up the package that had contained the underwear and she looked at the address. New York, New York.

Excitement licked at her stomach, yet it was laced with fear and Leila knew she could never do it.

Jasmine could have.

Jasmine would have.

Leila dressed in a gold robe and put on her veils and packed Jasmine's contents in the case and then walked back through the palace, past the portraits, past the lounge where her parents sat, no doubt speaking about Jasmine.

She wondered if they'd even notice that she had gone.

Leila told a servant to ring for a driver.

'Yalla!' Leila snapped, ordering him to hurry, and when a driver arrived she told him to take her to the airport.

Leila ordered a first-class ticket and held her breath as she handed over the card.

It worked.

It should have been a comfortable flight, but Leila could not relax and she declined when the steward offered to make up her bed.

Leila was tired, yet she would not sleep because she knew that it was then, and only then, that she cried.

Jasmine used to tease her about it, but there was no one to tease her now. Still Leila would wake in the midst of it sometimes, or in the morning her pillow would be wet and her eyes swollen, and the dreams, though all a bit different, all made her feel the same.

So, instead of sleeping, Leila selected a magazine and got goosebumps as she flicked through it and saw the bright lights of Times Square. It was hard to imagine that soon she herself would be there, for her life had been lived behind palace walls. Zayn had had more freedom, given that he was a male, and Jasmine had created her own, but Leila had never really ventured out.

Leila looked at an advert for a bar and saw pictures of cocktails in bright colours with tempting names. Even if she didn't really know what it was, she blushed when she saw there was one called Screaming Orgasm, and there were other names too, but she liked the look of one called Manhattan. She read about restaurants where people met just to talk and eat. She read about two luxury hotels in the heart of New York. The Chatsfield caught her eye. It had branches around the world and it would seem that the most scandalous and famous people stayed there.

There was talk of some rivalry between them and another hotel called The Harrington. It was glamorous and elegant and ensured privacy for its most esteemed guests.

She remembered the hotels when, having cleared customs, Leila found herself shivering in her robe on a cold winter night as she waited in line for a taxi. While others complained Leila patiently waited, her face to the heavens tasting snow on her tongue for the first time.

'Where to?' the driver asked.

Leila knew which one Jasmine would choose and she was about to say The Chatsfield, but changed her mind at the last moment.

'The Harrington,' Leila said.

Try as she might, Leila could never be Jasmine.

CHAPTER TWO

EVERYTHING WAS UNFAMILIAR.

Beautiful, yet unfamiliar.

Leila was grateful for her veils as she walked over to reception, for she felt as if everyone was looking at her.

Leila certainly turned heads—her gown was breathtaking. She held her back completely straight and asked to be taken to their very best suite.

It wasn't quite that easy though. There were many questions asked of her and Leila didn't answer all of them truthfully—she lied as to her address and just gave them a blank look when they asked for her phone number.

'I would just like to be taken to my suite.'

But still they asked more of her.

'Ms?'

Leila frowned at the receptionist's question.

'Your title?' the receptionist clarified. Leila glanced at her credit card and it read only as Leila Al-Ahmar, and she let out a breath as Leila realised that she could be whoever she wanted to be.

'Ms,' Leila said as her details were added to the computer. She handed over her credit card again, wondering if now her parents would have stopped it from working. The receptionist smiled at her, and handed her a swipe card for her suite, and Leila wondered if her parents had even bothered to notice that she'd gone.

When Leila stepped into the suite a maid was already in there, unpacking her small case, and Leila told her that she would not be needed.

She stood as if waiting for something.

'Dismissed,' Leila said. Once alone, she walked over to the window and looked to the busy streets below, trying to picture herself out there.

She couldn't.

She must.

Leila removed her robes and modest underwear and replaced it with Jasmine's. She did not recognise her own body, for in the mirror it was a wanton woman that looked back. She put on the black dress that revealed her cleavage and she struggled terribly to do up the zip at the back. She had never had a zip before and the maids did up her buttons. She added high shoes to her bare legs. Leila brushed her long black hair till it was gleaming. She had never worn make-up but tonight she carefully painted her lips and then stood back and gazed again at her reflection.

She could be Jasmine.

Yes, she was more slender than her sister had been and already she was a good few years older than Jasmine had been when she died. Yet, for the first time, she saw the resemblance to her older sister. Leila practised Jasmine's smile and wondered if their similarities were why her mother loathed her so much for living when Jasmine had died.

No, Leila reminded herself, her mother had loathed her from the second she was born.

Recalling her mother's words about the maids, Leila was hurt and angry enough to gather resolve and she stuffed her robe and veils into her small case and then hid it under the bed.

Princess Leila of Surhaadi no longer existed.

She had no bag to put the swipe card in and no maid to carry her things and so Leila tucked it into her bra.

The elevator took her down to the reception area and Leila looked around for a moment.

Elegance was the policy at The Harrington and famous people welcomed that they could be there without fuss. Such was her beauty though, such was her way, that people could not help but look around.

Leila was completely unused to being noticed or looked at and she was starting not to like it.

She heard the sound of a piano and followed it. As Leila walked into the bar, the chink of glasses and the sound of subdued conversation dimmed for a moment. She stood in the doorway in absolute terror, not that she showed it.

A portly man looked over and his eyes roamed Leila's body. Another man did the same, very briefly, but his eyes certainly flicked down to her breasts. It was so overwhelming for Leila she was about to turn tail and dash back to her suite. It had been a stupid idea, she decided. What the hell had she even been thinking?

But then *it* happened.

For the first time in her entire life, Leila felt welcome when she walked into a room. A man at the bar turned around and his chocolate-brown eyes met hers. For a brief second he startled and then frowned, as if trying to place her, and then he simply smiled.

Leila had never, not once, felt so welcome. His eyes did not roam her body as the other men's had; they simply met and held hers. Leila found that she was smiling back. Then, as naturally as breathing, she walked over to him.

'I've changed my mind,' the man said. His voice was rich and expensive and he turned and spoke to the barman. 'I shall have another drink after all.' Then his eyes returned to Leila's. 'What can I get you?'

'I don't know,' Leila said, and she looked at the glistening bottles of different colours and she did not feel naive. She felt looked after, for her vague response did not seem to faze him and he patiently waited for her to decide. She thought for a moment and remembered the cocktails she had seen in the magazine on the plane. Certainly wasn't going to ask for the one that made her blush! 'How about a Manhattan, given that is my first night here?'

'How about a *perfect* Manhattan,' he suggested, because that was what she was to him—utterly perfect. From her long glossy black hair to her golden eyes. The only thing he would change was the very bright lipstick she wore.

He would kiss it off soon, James knew that.

Bored by the subdued mood of The Harrington, James Chatsfield had been about to leave and head to somewhere more lively. He had just declined another drink when a hush had descended. Even the barman had paused mid-conversation with him and James had turned around and looked at a woman who could, upon entering, silence a room.

Leila nodded her consent to his drink selection and watched as the barman got to work but it did not hold her attention; instead it was the man who stood beside her, so she turned and looked at him

He was beautiful, with dark hair that fell to his collar. He was tall and well-dressed but there was a ruggedness to him that told

Leila he was untamed. There was an element to him that defied convention, for he was like no one else in the room. He wore a tie, yet the top of his shirt was unbuttoned. He was not clean shaven, yet he was clean—the scent of him told her that—and when he smiled, when she stood a little closer to him, his mere presence rendered her unafraid.

Her whole life she had been afraid, yet she wasn't now.

Her whole life she had taken up too much room merely by existing; now she stood by his side and peace somehow invaded.

'My name is James.'

'I am…' She was about to offer her title, but again changed her mind. 'I am Leila.'

She did not belong standing at a bar, James decided, and so he suggested that they move to one of the low tables. Leila chose one in the shadows not because she wanted to be more alone with him; she simply didn't want others' eyes on her. She sat on the sofa, expecting him to take a seat opposite, yet he came and sat beside her.

It wasn't invasive; there was distance but that he *chose* to come and sit by her side had her smile at him.

Their drinks were brought over and he watched as she took a sip and her eyes widened. She ran the tip of a pink tongue over her lips and then put her glass down.

'That tastes amazing,' Leila said. 'I can still feel it burning even though it tastes freezing.'

James, who usually needed to know so little about his sexual conquests, suddenly wanted to know every last thing about her.

'So this is your first night here?'

'It is.' Leila smiled. 'I have tasted snow as I waited for my taxi at the airport.'

'Why didn't you call me,' James said. 'I'd have come and got you.'

It was a silly thing to say perhaps, but it made so much sense to them both that Leila smiled. She felt as if they had been waiting for the other all their lives, as if she might have walked out of the airport and straight to his arms.

He asked her where she was from and James saw that she hesitated before answering.

'I am from Dubai,' Leila lied. 'I am here on business.'

'What sort of business are you in?'

It was a natural question but again she hesitated before answering, and James watched as one slender hand moved and tugged at her ear. 'I am a musician,' Leila said. 'I am here to see some performances.'

Liar, James wanted to say, for her cheeks dusted pink, though it was the oddest attempt at a lie that he had ever heard.

He didn't care that she lied though.

She just didn't have to lie to him, that was all.

James glanced at her hand and noted that she did not wear a ring, then he saw her long slender fingers. Perhaps she was not lying, for they were so long and delicate that possibly she should be stroking the ebony now.

'You?' Leila asked. 'What is it that you do?'

'Not an awful lot,' James admitted. 'My father calls me Jiminy.' When she frowned he elaborated. 'Jiminy Cricket.' Still she frowned and James realised she probably didn't know the song that he was referring to. 'He's a happy fellow who doesn't work very much,' James explained. 'I work for about half an hour a day making a fortune playing the stock markets and then I spend the next twenty-three and a half hours doing my level best to blow it.'

'And so what brings you here tonight?' Leila asked, taking another sip of her drink.

'I'm checking out the competition,' James said. 'I'm James Chatsfield…' He saw her nonplussed look. 'The Chatsfield hotels…' James further explained. His brother Spencer was determined to acquire The Harrington and had thought he had had the sale in the bag, but Isabelle Harrington, who was newly in charge, had unexpectedly knocked back the offer and things were starting to get extremely messy.

James was weary of his family; he wanted as far away from them as possible. Yet, idly curious, he had decided to drop in to The Harrington unannounced.

'My elder brother Spencer wants to buy this hotel. I decided to come and see for myself what all the fuss is about. I'm very glad now that I did.'

'I'm very glad that you did too,' Leila said.

He took one of her hands, the one nearest to the table, and Leila looked down as his fingers stroked hers. The contact was sublime —subtle but present, his fingers laced into hers—and she watched as their hands intertwined and their palms pressed together.

'I want to sip my drink,' Leila said, 'but I don't want to let go of your hand.'

'Then don't.' It was James who reached for her drink and brought it to her lips and she took a sip of it and felt his eyes on her throat as she swallowed.

'Actually, I do recognise the name,' Leila said, and her words brought his eyes back to hers. 'I think I read about your hotel on the plane.'

'It's not my hotel,' James said. 'I want nothing to do with the lot of them.'

'You have a lot of hotels?'

'I meant the family.' James smiled at the slight miscommunication. 'But yes, there are a lot of hotels. We have a very nice hotel in Dubai, but I haven't actually been there, though I might have to rectify that.' He gave her a flash of that depraved smile and then checked himself, for already, without even so much as a kiss, he was suggesting that they might be seeing each other again. For James, that was a no-no and so he quickly rectified things. 'Though perhaps not—Manu, the PR woman, has warned me my ways might not be welcome. Things are rather more strict there apparently…'

'Do you misbehave, James?' Leila asked, and he smiled at her curious question.

'That's a very nice way of putting it, but yes, I guess I do tend to misbehave.' She looked down to where his hand caressed hers and she was the bravest she had ever been— he made her so.

'Misbehave with me,' Leila whispered, terrified he might say no.

'God, yes.'

He released her hand although she wished he would not. She was not starved from his contact for long though, for he picked up a napkin and dipped it in some water. Leila frowned as his wrapped finger came towards her face, but she did not flinch and she did not move back.

'What are you doing?' Leila asked.

'Getting rid of the unnecessary,' James said. He usually preferred made-up women— he liked the mask, he liked the stranger—but he did not want that from Leila. He wanted her stripped, he wanted her naked, and that started now.

She liked the gentle pressure of his finger

on her lips. She liked the way his eyes narrowed as he concentrated on removing the lipstick from her mouth.

And concentrate he did.

'Now, you're perfect,' James said. 'Almost.'

'Almost?'

He went in his pocket and pulled out what Leila thought was another lipstick. 'What sort of man carries lipstick?' Leila asked, and he simply smiled as he got to work on her very full mouth.

'It's lip balm,' James corrected. 'If you ski as much as I do, you tend to carry it.'

She liked the waxy feel of it as he applied it. She ran her tongue over her lips and there was a slight taste of vanilla, but still she could not imagine her father or Zayn carrying such a thing.

For all her naivety Leila had not been completely shielded from men. She thought of Zayn's friends of yesteryear. Cocky playboys who used women, yet she did not feel used tonight. There was something else to James—something that made her smile, made her feel warm, made her feel very beautiful indeed, and that was something she had never felt before.

'You are like no one I have ever known,' Leila said.

'Snap.'

'Snap?' Leila checked, because even though her English was excellent she didn't know what that word meant.

'It means that I feel the same about you,' James said, and then he checked himself, because he didn't get involved in any one woman. He was saying things to Leila that he didn't usually say and he didn't want to give her mixed messages.

Tomorrow he would be gone.

'For now,' he amended.

'For now?'

'I'm very, very bad at relationships,' James said. 'I tend not to do them.'

'Tend?' Leila checked, for she did not understand that word also, but James took it that she wanted him to elaborate.

'I've had one serious relationship and she chose to go to the press and share every last thing that I'd told her in confidence as well as a lot of salacious details. What about you?' James asked. 'Have you ever been seriously involved with anyone?'

'Never,' Leila said.

She told the truth; James just never thought that she might mean literally.

More drinks were on the table, but it was not the liquor that made her giddy and laugh. It was this man who asked questions, who gave of himself, who laughed deeply and who simply could not release her hands save to feed her her drink.

'Do you want dinner?' James asked, but she shook her head for there was a different sort of hunger in Leila tonight and she told him that.

'I want to know about you.'

He revealed too much perhaps, but the gold of her eyes mesmerised and, even as he warned himself not to disclose it, James found himself telling Leila, warning her even, that he was a cad, a playboy, a rake. How he lived life his way, and it seemed to be working for he had the Midas touch when it came to the stock markets. How he partied at night, how he threw himself off mountains, how nothing and no one could tame him and how he chose not to impress.

'I tried behaving and I gave it up at the age of eighteen,' James said, and revealed how he had strived for perfection, but that noth-

ing he had ever done had been good enough
for his father.

He did not get sympathy from Leila.

'At least you were noticed,' Leila said. 'I
was ignored.'

'How could anyone ignore you?' James
asked. 'I don't believe it could be possible to
ignore you.'

'It's true,' Leila said. 'My mother…' She
hesitated. That her mother had never loved
her would surely make her unlovable to him.
That she had never, ever been wanted was her
deepest, darkest shame and so she bent history a little. 'Since Jasmine, my sister, died,
my mother has not been able to look at me,'
Leila said. 'And I have grown tired of waiting
and so now I do as I wish. I live as I want to.'

'They don't approve of that?'

'Oh, no, they don't approve,' Leila answered,

They never had.

'To two black sheep,' James said, and
raised another glass.

They were drinking shots now, saluting
their failures to measure up in their parents'
eyes. Knees were touching, eyes caressing
and, oh, it was the very best night of her life.

'So what,' Leila asked, for she could not ever get tired of getting to know this man, 'is your ambition? What do you aim for when everything you touch turns to gold? When you party all the time, when the world is at your feet, what do you strive for? What is it you want that you have never had?'

'You,' James said, and his mouth neared hers, but she knew that wasn't the full answer and Leila moved back her head.

'Tell me.'

'You wouldn't understand my answer,' James said.

'I might,' Leila said, 'or I might not, but either way I would love to hear it.'

She just might understand, James thought, and so he told her his truth. 'I want to know what it is to hit rock bottom,' James admitted, because maybe then he might feel…something.

'I already have,' Leila answered. Her life as she knew it was gone. Her family would disown her as surely as the sun would rise in the morning. Everything had sunk around her, but so long as she was here with James it simply did not matter as to the surroundings, for the night was beautiful. She looked to the man who had saved her from hell and his mouth was approaching hers. 'But I'm on my way up now,' Leila said.

Leila had never been kissed, she had really never even imagined being kissed, and yet now here it was—his mouth was soft and warm on hers. She did not move her lips to his at first, just relished the intimate weight, and when she saw that his eyes had closed, so, too, did hers.

And then her lips started to move and she was kissing him back softly, sliding her mouth over his. His hand captured her cheek and the other moved to her waist. She wanted to get closer to him, wanted to climb onto his lap; she wanted to be held in his arms.

Her lips parted, for no reason other than she wanted more of something she had never known, and James halted their kiss. Usually he did not care as to surroundings or discretion but she deserved better than his hand moving up her thigh, as it wanted to.

'Dance,' James said, his mouth just an inch from hers, aching in both of their groins.

'I don't want to dance,' Leila said, her eyes opening. 'I want to keep kissing.'

'Dance,' James said, for his body yearned

for more contact, and so he stood, and offered her his hand.

'I've never danced,' Leila admitted as they headed to the dance floor.

'I thought you said that you loved music.'

'I love to play it,' she admitted as he took her in her arms. 'I love to hear it...'

Now she got to feel it.

The slow sensual beat of the music was matched by the slow sensual caress of his body moving with hers. His face was in her hair and his arms loosely held her. His fingers stroked her bare arms and the shiver that ran through Leila had nothing to do with the temperature, for she had never been more warm.

'You smell amazing,' James said to her hair, and he pulled her in just a little closer, but enough that she felt his hardness. The nudge of his erection on her stomach had her giddy, had her damp, had her mouth move to find his.

'Not here,' James said, denying her another kiss, and he offered what he hoped she would not want. 'We can go to a bar I know, if you think here is a bit staid...'

Staid?

She had never been wilder in her life. She

was moving to music, pressed to a man whose body made hers ache with suspense.

'Or,' James carefully suggested, 'we could go back to The Chatsfield…' he offered, for it was where he usually took women. Never back to his penthouse, which made things too personal. But, James decided, if she declined his offer, he might even suggest they go there, so desperate was he to have her, but her response most pleasantly surprised him.

'Can we go to my suite?' Leila asked, for she was looking at his mouth, feeling his warmth, and she craved for it to be just the two of them, to finally be alone with him.

Hearing her ask to retire to her suite now had him wonder if an angel had just fallen from heaven.

'We can,' James said.

'One more dance though,' Leila said, for she did not want to leave his arms for even a moment.

It was music she had never heard before but it was etched to her heart now, for with each sway, with each breath, he brought her to somewhere she did not know existed. Her breasts ached, her thighs at the top ached too, and at her very centre she needed more of him. Her mouth yearned for his and his fingers, now gently exploring her spine through her dress, made her feel naked and produced a sudden tension in her.

'I need your kiss,' Leila said, and James looked right back at her.

There was no language barrier to her words; she spoke the truth.

'Now,' Leila said, and her voice was a touch urgent.

'Don't you want to dance some more?' James said, for she was so close he could feel it building in her and so he whispered into the shell of her ear. 'A musician that's never danced,' James murmured. 'That must have taken some restraint.'

She was glad, so glad, he was holding her, for without him she would simply sink to her knees. She answered him with a truth that had him lead her from the dance floor.

'I have no restraint tonight.'

CHAPTER THREE

THANK GOD THEY were alone in the elevator, for they kissed the way a couple should only kiss when alone.

Their mouths belonged to each other, his hands pressed at her buttocks and he ground his pelvis into her. The ache he procured deepened, his erection something she needed to feel, yet even with it pressed hard into her groin it was not enough.

They made it halfway along the corridor to her suite, then he kissed her up against the wall. Her hands pressed his head into hers and like conjoined crabs they walked sideways kissing to her door.

'Where's...?' James said to her mouth, for he remembered that she did not have a bag with her and they needed the swipe card to her door so badly.

'In my bra,' Leila mumbled, and his hand slid to the wrong breast and it lingered, stroking her to the edge of orgasm, then moving over to the other. He retrieved the warm card and opened the door and barely registered their surrounds as he shrugged off his jacket. He simply had eyes only for her.

Leila's hands went to her back to undo the zip of her dress and, seeing her breasts jut and her struggle to be naked for him, when first he had wanted Leila up against the wall and inside her this moment, James turned her around instead.

'*I'm* undressing you,' James said with command, for it could very easily be over in a moment, yet he wanted to take his time.

Leila's maid usually undressed her.

But not like this.

He placed her palms to the wall and she rested her head on it. With every inch the zip lowered down her spine, her skin was caressed by his tongue. Down, slowly down with the zipper, until, on his knees, he kissed the small of her back and she shivered as his jaw scratched her soft skin and his hand moved up between her legs. Her tiny panties were damp and Leila let out a moan as his fingers slid inside and she gasped as he located a spot that she had never even known existed.

'How do you know…?' she begged as he continued to bring her to life with his touch. Her thighs were like water and his mouth was leaving her back now, his hold on her easing as he shifted position.

'Don't stop,' Leila begged, but he stood and removed her palms from the wall and turned her around.

'We're not stopping,' James said, for there were still six hours left of their one night. He discarded her dress and Leila felt free. Free to stand in her underwear and heels and watch him admire her.

His thumb stroked the red velvet of her bra and she watched her already erect nipples grow under his touch, then bit on her lip as his mouth suckled her through the fabric.

'Please…' Leila begged. It was the nicest thing she had ever experienced, yet it was still not enough.

'Slow down,' James said, words he rarely did.

Were it not Leila he'd have had her by now, would be deep inside her, taking her up against the wall. The temptation to do so was still there, still strong…

Yes, it was there but instead he was teasing out a dark nipple, caressing it with his mouth, and the moans from Leila were worth his rare restraint. The scent of her hair was the same as her skin—rare, exotic and oiled—and so he lingered.

She was shocked that a man might suck from her breast, but it was so sublime that she pleaded for more when he stopped.

'James…' His mouth left her breast and it left it cold, swollen and aching, yet his mouth did not leave her skin. Standing she endured his deep kiss down her stomach. Yes, endure, Leila thought as she stood there almost weeping. It felt like hunger, it felt like sin, it felt delicious what his kiss could do.

'This isn't sex…' Leila whimpered as he slid down her panties and he probed her with his tongue. This wasn't like the pictures in the palace library that she had peeked at a few times and had made her forbidden place feel warm.

'Do you want me to stop?' James asked, his mouth hovering over her clitoris, his breath warm and tempting.

Leila answered him with her hand, pressing his head back into her, and for a moment she stared down. One breast was exposed, the other covered by fabric made wet by his mouth. Her stomach was not familiar, for beneath it was his hair, and the noise of his intimate explorations had her moaning.

'James…' She wanted him to stop, yet she did not. His mouth was soft, yet she had never felt anything more intense. Her thighs were shaking; his hand clamped her buttocks so there was no escape from his relentless tongue and the soft sucking noises he made. When he moaned into her mound, everything gathered, every nerve pointed and shot to her centre. Leila thought she would topple, but instead the wall supported her back and his arms pressed her groin to his face as she came shockingly, wickedly, deliciously.

The warning that he was close to coming himself had him pull back and look up at her as she slowly opened her eyes and met his.

'My turn now,' Leila said, and he smiled at her back-to-front way of thinking. 'I want to see you.'

His shirt had too many buttons, Leila decided, for she was very bad at undoing buttons when the maids usually did it for her. She tried to kiss his chest as he had her back, but she grew impatient and tore the bottom of his shirt open instead. 'You are beautiful,' Leila said, for he was—his pale skin was toned and his nipples were the same dark red of his mouth and deserved tasting. So, too, did his stomach; the snake of hair there as she undid his belt was rough to her mouth. She could feel his erection straining beneath the fabric against her cheek and for a moment she kissed him through it, then she pushed up from her knees to stand.

Nothing scared her; he only made her curious. The way his cock sprang to greet her as she freed it, the way he moaned as she ran her fingers along its length. She pressed her free hand into his mouth and he suckled on her fingers as he stepped out of trousers and then she stopped touching him, for Leila did not like his socks.

'Take them off,' Leila instructed, and it was said with such authority and command James half expected her to produce a whip.

'Do you like giving orders, Leila?' James asked, removing the offending garments.

'It comes very naturally to me.' Leila nodded.

'Not tonight it doesn't,' James said. 'Take off your bra.'

It was half off already but she did not comply. 'Remove it for me.'

They stood in a delicious stand-off and with a wry smile he tugged it around and removed the clasp and dropped it to the floor.

'Get on the bed,' James said.

She could not breathe, no air would go in and no air would come out. She liked the command of his voice and even though he was stern it did not feel like being told off.

'Get on the bed, Leila...' James said. 'It can be your turn tomorrow.'

What the hell was he talking about tomorrow for? James wondered. He picked up his jacket and took out some condoms as the beguiling beauty finally complied and got on the bed. Naked, Leila lay there; every cell in her body thrummed in anticipation and she told him how she felt. 'I want to writhe beneath you...' Then she stopped as she saw he was putting a sheath on. She knew a little and she also knew that she did not like that ugly pink thing.

'Take it off,' Leila said. 'I'm on the pill.'

James stood there; he was the most careful

of careful but he'd long since lost his head to-night. When he did not obey her instruction, when he stood by the bed, Leila removed it for him and lowered her head and licked him. 'I will take away the taste of plastic...'

She wanted back to the musky scent of him and she licked along his length. Leila licked her tongue around the shaft, working her way to his head, tasting and swallowing the thin stream that came from the delicious tip with a mounting pleasure. She felt his hand on her head as he guided her to take it fully in, but she was enjoying simply licking him. Then suddenly she toppled as James pushed her back onto the bed and as he came over her she felt his impatience and power. His mouth crushed hers and as his thigh parted hers, Leila opened her legs readily. The weight of him on top of her was pure pleasure and the harshness of his kiss and the roughness of his jaw took her higher. The swollen feel of him there at her entrance served as poor warning for the absolute pain as he seared in, tearing her, parting her in one deft thrust, and she arched into him and let out a scream.

What the...? James stilled. He'd never had a virgin before, but there was no mistaking he was having one now. She was incredibly tight around him and he'd taken her with such force that he'd been unable to halt. 'I hurt you…'

'That was not hurt,' Leila whispered. Hurt was a world without him, hurt was a lifetime of being ignored. She placed her hand over his buttock and did not like that she was without his kiss and her mouth sought his.

'You should have told me…' James said.

'I did,' Leila said. 'I told you I had never…'

He'd run out of questions; all he could feel was her wrapped tight around him and the slight pressure of her hand that told him to go on. He moved back a little and then in again, and it must have hurt her because James could see tears in her eyes and her teeth gritting. He moved up on one elbow and put an arm beneath her head to have her mouth more accessible to him. He kissed her as he had never kissed another and Leila's heart knew it. He kissed away the pain as he moved just a little inside her. Not the pain down below, for there was bliss coming back there now. His lips made up for every slight, for every cruel word that had been said, and he was better than music, for Leila knew then that love existed.

His hesitation diminished as her body started to move to his. He moved his arm so her head dropped back to the mattress and her hips started to lift. Her moans of pleasure, Leila realised, drove him on. So, too, did the lift of her groin. Faster and harder he moved as her body willed his to and then when he could surely not fill her anymore, he swelled further.

And it was then she found it.

The place she had always been seeking. It was navy and silver and she entered that place with James.

He saw it, too, as he shot into her.

It was all he could see as she sobbed out his name and her tight space clenched around him over and over as he filled her.

She loved the collapse of him on top of her and the twitch of both of them after, sated but still sensitive, as they came back to the world together.

He had a million questions but there was not one he could think of now because nothing really mattered as they kissed and then lay there.

'Go to sleep,' James said, because he could feel her soft and exhausted, and her eyelashes were blinking on his chest as she fought to keep her eyes open.

Instead she lay there pretending to be asleep until he was.

She did not want to cry out, even though Leila was quite sure that she would not tonight for she had never felt such peace in her life. It wasn't just the sex; it was the feel of his arm around her and the rise of his chest as he breathed beneath her cheek.

It was the bliss of finally being held in another's arms; it was contact. And now she had it she would stay awake forever if she had to, just to revel in this.

And stay awake Leila did till morning. James stirred and her face turned to his chest and she tasted again the salty skin. Her hand slid down and she closed her fingers around the solid length that had driven her to new places in the night, felt again its power and her kiss to his chest deepened.

James's hand came over hers for a moment, guiding her slow movement, giving in to the sensations.

James didn't, as a rule, like morning sex.

It was too intimate; it promised too much and it was promising it now.

He wanted to turn, wanted to lift her chin and kiss her; he wanted his hand that was stroking her buttocks to slip between her legs and part her and take her again.

He was that close to doing that, but last night's many questions were making themselves known now, and he told Leila that he was going to take a shower.

The mirror told the tale.

His chest was bruised by her mouth and his hangover was starting to catch up with him. One cocktail too many, James thought as he stepped into the shower. That, he was used to, but as James looked down and saw the smear of blood at the top of his thighs, it wasn't his hangover that was troubling him—one virgin was one virgin too many for him.

That, he *wasn't* used to.

He reached for soap and looked around; he liked the clues of a woman's bathroom. He expected exotic fragrances, for her hair had smelled divine, but it was just the exclusive toiletries synonymous with The Harrington.

Out of the shower he wrapped his hips in a

towel and opened a hotel toothbrush and that niggle that something didn't sit right started to multiply.

No woman, *no* woman he had ever been with, possessed so little. There was a hairbrush and a small toiletry bag with a lipstick and, *thank God*, James thought, there was a packet of contraceptive pills.

His businesswoman from Dubai sure travelled light.

Leila watched as he came out of the shower. She could see the tense set of his unshaven jaw as he walked towards the large fitted wardrobe.

'What are you doing?'

'Just getting a robe.'

James pulled one from the hangers but he wasn't there for a robe; instead he had confirmed his suspicions, for there were no clothes, no shoes, no bags.

Nothing.

Instead of putting on the robe he dried himself and looked over to the mystery woman who lay in bed.

Was she a journalist? James wondered. They were all over him at the moment. God knows he'd told her far too much last night.

Had Isabelle hired her as some sort of plant when she'd heard that James was at the hotel? That would make more sense because Isabelle would do anything to discredit the Chatsfield name.

'Do you want to go down for breakfast?' James said.

'We could have it here,' Leila answered, for she knew she could not put on last night's dress and shoes.

'Why don't we go somewhere,' James pushed, and Leila stared back. Her eyes felt gritty from a lack of sleep, and as she looked at James she started to realise that whatever they had found last night had gone.

'Come on,' James said, 'let's go down for breakfast.' He wanted her to tell him that her luggage had been delayed, he wanted her to tell him her reasons, yet Leila did not.

'Why are you getting dressed?' Leila asked.

'I've got a meeting at nine,' James said.

It was just after six.

He was actually conflicted.

For the most part he did not want to leave, yet it wasn't just getting involved with her, or even her innocence, that unnerved him, but her deception.

He simply couldn't leave it there though. It would seem for Leila he broke every rule.

'Call me…' James said, writing down his cell phone number and putting it by her bedside. 'Give me your number…'

'My number?'

'Your cell phone.'

'I don't have one…' Leila said, and then remembered she was supposed to be a businesswoman from Dubai and of course she would have a cell phone. 'I mean, I don't have it to hand…'

'Of course you don't,' James said tartly, and then finished dressing and left.

No, angels did not fall from heaven.

CHAPTER FOUR

SHE HAD BEEN worth the trouble he now found himself in.

The stars that James saw, as his head was slammed against a wall, were not dissimilar to the ones he had glimpsed that night all those weeks ago with Leila.

For a second the world was a deep navy, with glimpses of silver.

It consisted of nothing more than that.

James closed eyes and took in the simple scenery and would rather have liked to stay there but an angry voice was demanding his return.

A night, such as the one he and Leila had shared, could not come without consequence, James thought, and now here it was.

That's right, James remembered as he opened his eyes to hostility, he was in an alley behind

The Chatsfield and about to be beaten to within an inch of his life by the Royal Prince Zayn Al-Ahmar of Surhaadi for deflowering his sister.

He'd known that Leila was lying from the very start.

He understood why a little better now.

No wonder she had needed to escape, James thought, for Zayn spoke of possession and dishonouring not just Leila but the royal family and his people.

'That's a very heavy burden to place on one woman's body,' James responded to Zayn's furious rant, and got a hand around his throat as a reward for his words, but it didn't stop him speaking. 'I was not aware that the integrity of the nation rested upon your sister's maidenhead.'

'You have no place to comment on integrity,' Zayn said, and James felt the grip tighten around his throat. 'You are a man in possession of none.'

Zayn was wrong. James had had integrity around Leila—he simply could not discard her. After he had left her that morning he'd barely made it till nine before he'd caved and sent flowers, asking her to call him.

He'd sent more flowers the next day and the next and yet Leila still hadn't responded to him. He'd caved again and called The Harrington, but that they were so discreet combined with the fact he didn't even know her surname had meant that they would neither confirm nor deny that she was staying there.

He found himself at her door once but had attempted to let go of the madness and turned around.

In the end James had taken himself off to France for a spot of skiing, determined to screw his way out of it, but all roads led to Leila in the erection stakes. He'd danced, he'd kissed, he'd been his flirtatious, outrageous best, but nothing with another produced even a stirring. Rather than destroy his formidable reputation with a no-show in *that* department he'd returned each night to his luxurious cabin alone.

And thought of Leila. How they had sat and talked for hours, how easily it had been to open up to the other.

How, for a while there, as they had drank shots and celebrated being the two black sheep, they had felt the same.

He looked at her brother and James was angry for her.

'At least I don't treat women like they are my property.'

'Perhaps not, Chatsfield, but the fact remains that you have badly handled what belongs to me. My family, anyone beneath my protection, belongs to me. You are fortunate we are *not* in my country, for there, I would not hesitate to remove the member that committed the offence.'

Offence?

There had been nothing remotely offensive about that night. It had stayed with James for weeks now. An offence might have occurred if the seduction hadn't been so mutual. James could very well have pointed out that Leila had been a very willing participant in the supposed downfall of her country, but he chose not to make this salacious comment.

Instead he shrugged Zayn off in one easy motion and told him a few other home truths—that Zayn was positively biblical. When Zayn warned him never to repeat what had happened, nor to let it out in the press, James merely laughed in his face and told him that he didn't need the publicity. That here in New York the Chatsfields were royalty.

Fighting down some back alley was an experience James did not need and so he walked away from it.

Winded from the fight, he would not let Zayn see that and only when he got onto the street did he take a moment to get his breath.

His hands went to his pocket, checking for his wallet and keys, but instead they closed around a tube of lip balm and his mind went straight back to Leila.

A princess!

Despite his nonchalant responses to the threats, James was starting to realise the enormity of what he had done.

James headed for home, to his luxurious penthouse that overlooked Central Park, and he eyed the damage in the mirror.

There were finger marks around his neck, a bruise to his eye and the size of the lump on the back of his head probably meant that he should get checked out by a doctor.

Instead James poured himself a whisky and lay on the bed, pondering his next move.

He picked up his phone to check, and no, she hadn't called him.

Leila was the one woman who didn't.

He'd thought her a journalist, or that it might be a set-up by Isabelle. Instead she was a princess and her family was clearly incensed by what had taken place. He just hoped she was okay and that he'd been the sole receiver of Zayn's fury.

Why would she have told her brother? He hoped to God she wasn't pregnant, but she had been on the pill—James had seen them for himself. James was quite certain from Zayn's fury that, had he got the precious princess pregnant, then he'd have been told about it, just before he took his dying breath! He lay there brooding, wondering why Leila would have told her brother what had gone on between them. The more he thought about that night, the clearer it became to him that Leila had walked into that bar with one thing on her mind. She'd used him, perhaps, to get out of marriage. No doubt the Al-Ahmars wanted her kept a virgin.

James lay there, angry at her, used by her, hard for her.

Five lots of flowers!

He could imagine her rolling her eyes when she took the deliveries.

Loser.

Well, he wasn't going to spend time looking over his shoulder, waiting to see what sort of further punishment Zayn had in mind for him.

He'd wasted enough time over Leila, waiting for her to call.

James pulled out his case and he thought of all the women he *hadn't* been with since that one night. He didn't like that he had become so pensive, didn't like how hung up he was on Leila.

He took out a shirt; it was the one he had worn that night and her exotic scent still clung to it. James buried his head in it for a moment and inhaled her. He was hard for her still.

Time to take care of that, James decided.

But rather than returning to the bed and his memories as he had these past weeks, he tossed the shirt back to the floor of the wardrobe and packed his case and decided on a return to France and the snowy slopes.

There was still some of the *screwing* season left after all!

CHAPTER FIVE

As HANGOVERS WENT, this was a particularly bad one.

James sat on the terrace of the ski resort behind dark glasses and took a very welcome sip of strong, sweet coffee as he eyed the magnificent view.

He looked over to the black run that he would hurl himself down later.

At least it would clear his head.

Last night had been a particularly heavy one. Some idiot had hired a flash mob to take over the bar to assist in his wedding proposal. The man had clearly needed every assistance because the poor woman had, to James, looked as if she wanted to run.

Without the onlookers, James was quite sure that she would have said no to him.

Instead James had watched as the man had

dropped to his knees and asked her if they could return here next year on their—wait for it, James thought—honeymoon!

'How romantic,' a leggy blonde woman beside him had said.

How awful, James had privately thought, though he hadn't said that. Instead he had bought Longlegs a drink.

And another.

He was like a repeat prescription, James thought as he sat there recovering the next morning.

He resisted opening the American newspaper that had been pre-emptively placed on his table, for usually he requested one.

Just not today.

James really didn't want to see himself leaving the club with yet another glossy blonde.

What was her name?

Certainly it wasn't Leila, because when this morning he'd inadvertently called her that, it had earned him a slap to the cheek.

Christ.

He'd tried to ski his way out of it, tried to screw his way out of it, but still every morning he woke hard for Leila.

Every night was an attempt to relive that one.

Not just the sex, although it was a lot about the sex. Still he kept remembering the moment she had walked into the bar.

His ex, who had gone to the press with his stories, had taken months just to get some salacious tidbits out of him. He'd spoken so readily with Leila.

She hadn't with him though, James remembered.

He'd been used; James knew that much.

He could have been anyone.

Rather than think about it James opened up the paper and took another sip of coffee as he turned to the business section.

Then something caught his eye and he almost spat out his coffee.

There was Leila, dressed in finery, her head and mouth covered, but it was certainly her, for he would never forget those eyes.

And there, looking far less than regal, was a very tacky shot of himself and some blonde making out at the bar.

All this he took in as he sat there, his mind choosing to linger on the images than focus on the headline, but then not even James could ignore what was written.

Princess Leila Al-Ahmar of Surhaadi was

three months pregnant and, according to extremely reliable sources, the father was none other than James Chatsfield.

He looked at the caption beneath the image of himself and a woman.

James Chatsfield celebrating the happy news!

It never even entered his head that he might not be the father.

Oh, she'd used him that night, all right.

He picked up his phone and scrolled through it and called The Harrington, his temper mounting as, thanks to their bloody discretion, they still refused to even confirm or deny if Leila was staying there.

'Put me through now,' James shouted to the receptionist. 'I know that she's staying there, and I don't care if it's the middle of the bloody night—you will put me through now.'

But again he was politely reminded of The Harrington's policy on guest confidentiality and it dawned on James that she possibly wasn't there. He looked back at the newspaper and acknowledged that this might not be some library image the paper had produced. She could be back in Surhaadi now.

Pregnant with *his* child.

His phone rang and James saw that it was Spencer but he ignored it; he did not need a lecture from his brother right now.

He needed to know how to deal with Leila and so he called Manu in Dubai, the only person he could think of who might be able to help. 'What do you know about Surhaadi, about their royals?'

'Not a lot, but I'd guess that right now you wouldn't be their favourite person,' Manu tartly answered. 'She's a royal princess, James, from an extremely conservative country. I would imagine they'll close ranks around her and she won't be seen in public from this point on. I certainly wouldn't be holding my breath for an invitation to dinner to get to know the grandparents. What the hell were you thinking?'

'I wasn't thinking,' James snapped. 'Leila was the one doing that.' James was quite certain of it now.

'You're saying she set out to trap you...' Manu gave an incredulous laugh. 'I don't think she needs money to support her child.'

'It wasn't about money,' James said, re-membering her walking into the bar that night. 'I could have been anyone…'

'Poor James,' Manu mocked him. They didn't get on, they never had. Manu thoroughly disapproved of his ways. 'I'm sure there are many women applauding the fact that you're getting a taste of how it feels to be used.'

'I think she did this to get out of some marriage…'

'Very possibly.'

'What rights would I have?'

'Rights!' Manu gave another incredulous laugh. 'You lost any right to a fair hearing from them long ago, James. The best I can suggest is that you attempt to sort things out with Leila before she returns there.'

'She's not gone back?'

'Apparently she's still at The Harrington,' Manu said. 'I just came off the phone with Spencer. He's freaking out.'

'I know,' James said, 'he's trying to get through to me now.' He rang off and took the call from Spencer.

'This is a PR nightmare!' Spencer shouted.

'Have you any idea the damage that this is causing?'

'Oh, and there I was thinking you were ringing to congratulate me,' came James's sarcastic response.

'Have you seen the papers?' Spencer sneered. 'There's nothing in them deserving of congratulations.'

'I know.' James let out a breath—it really was an appalling mess.

'It gets better,' Spencer continued with his rant. 'Rumour has it that your little princess's credit card has been stopped by her family. Probably in attempt to force her to come home.'

'Who told you that?'

'I've got my spies at The Harrington,' Spencer said. 'I haven't got to the best bit yet. Isabelle, out of the goodness of her heart, or rather to completely discredit us, is going to let your pregnant princess stay there for nothing. It's the least she can do apparently.' Spencer let out an angry breath. 'Sort it, James.'

'I intend to.'

'God knows how. You know how much this means to me. You know I'm doing everything I can to show Gene I can run the place.'

'Right now,' James said, 'I couldn't give a damn about The Chatsfield.'

'You never have. You only care about yourself, James, I get that. Know this much though—I am not letting the Chatsfield reputation slide just because you can't keep it in your pants. Sort it,' Spencer said again, and rung off.

James took a helicopter to the airport and then had an hour to kill before his flight back to New York.

He rang The Harrington but again they refused to put him through.

She couldn't hide from him forever.

Oh, yes, she could, a small inner voice said—she was a royal princess from a foreign land.

Eight hours' flying time did nothing to improve James's temper. New York was wet and grey and the cold sheets of rain meant that his driver could only move the car slowly through the heavy traffic.

Thanks to the time difference, the day that brought him to her was lasting forever.

He told his driver to take his luggage to his home and then to come and wait here for him. He strode through the foyer of The Harrington and James punched the elevator. He didn't care if they'd changed her room; he'd knock on every door if he had to.

'Sir, only guests staying here can use the elevators…' A very worried concierge who'd been warned to be on the lookout for James Chatsfield was racing towards him.

'Tough!' James said as the elevator doors closed.

It was the same one they had made out in, James knew that, though he did his level best not to think about that night now.

They must have alerted Leila that he was on his way up because as he strode down the corridor her door opened and there she stood.

He'd built her up to be some kind of shrew, some Desdemona, yet she stood dressed in a white hotel robe and such was her beauty he knew there and then why he hadn't been able to get over her.

She was thinner than he remembered and there were dark smudges under her eyes, but they did not meet his. Those once-pretty lips were pursed but she prised them open to give her orders.

'I will come down and speak with you in

the dining room,' Leila said. 'You will wait for me there.'

'You don't give me orders, Leila,' James said.

'I'm not even dressed…'

'You've got far more on now than you did that night,' James said, and he pushed past the door and into her suite. 'Remember that night, Leila, the night you set out to get pregnant…?'

'I did not,' Leila said. 'I was on the pill.'

'Please…' He looked at her, remembered her very deliberately removing the condom, and then he tried not to remember that.

Leila stood with her heart hammering in her chest as James took a seat in a leather chair.

'We're going to talk.'

'I need to get dressed.'

He stood, lifted the chair and moved it to the bedroom doors, which he left open. He turned the chair around, so he faced outwards. 'Get dressed then, but I'll hear if you open a window,' James said. 'And, once dressed, you and I are going to have a very long talk.'

The phone rang and Leila looked at it, but

James, who knew hotels better than most, told her who it would be.

'That will be reception checking to see if you're okay and if you want me removed from your suite.'

'I want you removed,' Leila said.

'Well, you'd better tell them to send the police then, because the only way they'll take me out is cuffed. Like it or not we *are* going to talk, Leila. It might as well be now.'

She answered the phone and looked at the back of his head. Leila could see the tense set of his shoulders, yet she didn't really fear him as such.

She just feared the conversation ahead.

Leila let out a breath and chose to face it. 'I'm fine,' she said to the worried receptionist. 'You don't need to send anyone.'

'Tell them to send afternoon tea because we're going to be here some time.' James turned his head but she ignored that request and put down the phone.

'Get dressed,' he said.

Leila went to her closet and tried to decide what to wear. She found western clothes very confusing and longed for robes, but she had only brought one with her.

Oh, what to wear?

'Leila…' James warned as she took her time.

He was here to discuss the business of their child so Leila selected a black linen suit that she had seen the beautiful business-women wearing as she sat in Central Park and watched the world go by.

She laid it out on the bed and then opened a drawer and looked for underwear and a top that would go with the suit. She could hear him tapping his foot in impatience but Leila refused to be rushed.

It was more than impatience; he knew she had undone her robe and he was fighting instinct not to turn around.

Leila felt strange having him here in the room as she dressed, for she remembered the heat of their *un*dress.

She pulled on panties that she had bought in Macy's when her card had still been working. Then she pulled on a little silver top that she had bought there too.

'How long does it take to get dressed, Leila?'

'It takes me a considerable time,' Leila answered. 'I'm not used to dressing myself and neither am I used to buttons.'

He tried not to smile and then he grimaced as he remembered her tearing off his shirt.

'Are you dressed yet?'

'I haven't tied back my hair,' Leila said.

His patience ran out and he stood. As she picked up her hairbrush James removed it from her hand and put it on the dresser and for the first time today they met the other's eye.

'The hair is fine,' James said. 'We're going to talk now.'

Not yet, James realised, as there was a knock at the door.

He knew it would be someone to discreetly check if she was okay.

It was.

'I would tell you if I wanted to be disturbed,' Leila said rudely, and James raised his eyebrows at the tone of her voice and wondered where the woman he had met all those weeks ago had gone. 'Dismissed.'

She closed the door and turned to James.

'Take a seat at the table,' he told her.

Unlike the night they had met, he sat opposite her. When he spoke, his voice was not kind as it once had been.

'No lies, Leila. You are going to tell me the truth…'

'I don't lie.'

'Oh, is that so,' James said, 'Ms travelling musician from Dubai.'

'I like music.'

'Did you set out to get pregnant?'

Leila looked at him. 'No.'

'I said no lies!' James was doing his best not to shout.

'I am not lying. I would never choose this—I vomit all the time. It is the most horrible thing to happen to me…' Her eyes reproached him as if he was the cause of it.

Which he was, of course, but… 'You told me you were on the pill.'

'I was,' Leila said. 'James, I did not set out to get pregnant.'

'So what did you set out for?' James asked.

'I ran away,' Leila admitted, and she looked at the man who had taken her heart the night she had run, and she hated him for walking out the next day.

'Why didn't you tell me that you were pregnant?'

'You seemed busy with your blonde women,' Leila sneered.

Busy trying to get over you, James thought, though he didn't tell her that.

'Yep, I was also busy being beaten up in dark alleys.'

'I apologise for my brother's violence towards you. If it makes you feel any better, I am not speaking to him now,' Leila said. It wasn't just for that reason though that Leila wasn't speaking to her brother—Zayn had called Leila last night to warn her that the news of her pregnancy would break today and that the father would be named. He had also told her that he was no longer marrying the woman he had been betrothed to. In fact, the woman he was seeing now, Sophie, was the journalist who had revealed James's name to the press.

'Who else did you tell?' James asked.

'No one.'

'So how do the papers know?'

'Perhaps the doctor…'

'Oh, and did the doctor ask you your lover's name?'

He blocked every exit with his cool stare. 'No,' Leila said, gulping.

'So, who else did you tell?'

'I told no one apart from my brother.'

'Still she lies,' James said, because someone must have spoken to the media. 'Well, your brother omitted to mention that you were pregnant when he had his hands around my throat. I'm assuming that he knew then.'

Leila closed her eyes. 'Yes, he tracked me down a few weeks ago and I told him that I was with child and that I didn't know what to do…'

'And yet, you didn't think to ring me. Instead you sent him to beat me up.'

There was a long stretch of silence before Leila spoke. 'It's complicated, James,' Leila said instead. 'Zayn is very protective towards me.'

'Actually, it's not complicated at all,' James interrupted. 'We had sex, and now we're having a baby…' It was starting to dawn on him that this was real. 'You had no right, no right at all, to keep this news from me. Was I ever going to find out?'

'I tried to call you.'

'Liar.'

'I did,' Leila said. 'That number you gave me was wrong.'

'No, it wasn't.'

'It was,' Leila said. 'I tried many times to call you.'

'Try it now,' James challenged.

He stood and so, too, did Leila and she took the number from a drawer and walked over to a walnut desk. James watched as she dialled the number and closed his eyes in brief frustration as she had omitted to dial for an outside line.

'Are you kidding me, Leila?'

'Kidding?' Leila frowned.

'You really don't know how to get an outside line?' He saw her blink and then frown in confusion.

'I just press three and ask for my meals to be sent to me.'

She went back and sat at the table. 'I know you think I was trying to trap you but I truly was not. In many ways it has been good not being able to speak with you because I've been able to work through things myself and I've given it a lot of thought. I am angry with my brother about the fight, and anyway, I don't want to rely on him or anyone. I am going to raise my baby alone.'

'Our baby,' James corrected, and Leila felt

her throat constrict when she heard the snap of possession in his voice.

'I don't need your help in this, James.'

'It's not about what *you* need. It's about what the baby needs,' James said. 'Though I'd suggest that you do need some help. I've heard on the grapevine that your credit card has been stopped. I guess Mommy and Daddy are not very amused with their daughter's behaviour.'

'I don't think that they will ever speak with me again,' Leila said, 'so I doubt I will find out.'

James looked at her and felt a bit bad then—his parents were trouble enough but Leila was dealing with a king and queen. 'I'm sure they'll come around.'

He took a breath; a sense of disquiet was growing as the ramifications of that thought hit home. Yes, her parents would surely come around and what then?

What happened then to the princess and her baby?

What happened to *his* child?

'How did your parents take the news?' Leila asked.

'I'm not here to talk about our families,'

James said. 'I'm here to sort things out between us.'

'There is no us,' Leila said.

'Who's your OB?' James asked, and she frowned. 'Your physician? You have seen someone other than the hotel doctor?'

'No.'

'You haven't had an ultrasound?' James checked, and she simply stared back at him. 'It might be twins!'

'There are a lot of twins in my family.'

The day just got better and better!

'So, Leila, what are you going to do for money now that your parents have cut you off?' James asked, and glanced around the room. He'd seen in the bedroom when he'd stood from the chair that her once-empty wardrobe was now bulging and there was a lot of evidence of her extravagance here too—she must have fifty bottles of perfume laid out on the table and the diamonds sparkling from her ears hadn't been there that night.

Her make-up was amazing though—her lips were in a neutral shade much more subtly seductive than that terrible red lipstick she had worn, and the touch of mascara she wore now accentuated the gold of her eyes.

'What I do for money is not your concern.'

'Actually, it is,' came James's sarcastic response, 'because given the news you're no doubt entitled to half of mine...'

'James,' Leila interrupted. 'I know there are laws here, that you will feel obligated, but I told you, I have already decided to go it alone. Anyway, I don't want someone so promiscuous or reckless as a father...'

'Don't. You. Dare!'

Leila shivered as she heard James, the man who had once made her smile, now speak in ice. The man whose voice had once soothed her now made her stomach clench.

'Don't you dare try to exclude me from my child's life. I'm not one of your servants that you can dismiss.'

'Actually,' Leila coolly said, and James's mouth gaped, 'you are.'

She got up and walked over to the table. She picked up the newspaper and tossed it to him, and then she opened a drawer and took out some magazines she'd spent a lot of time crying over and she tossed them at him too.

Then Leila picked up the phone and dialled three.

'I would like James Chatsfield removed now.'

'Tell them that I'm already leaving,' James said, and stood. He was struggling to stay calm. She was like no one he had ever dealt with, but there was no way that he'd let her simply remove him from his own child's life.

'I will call you later, Leila,' James said. 'And I very much suggest that you pick up the phone.'

As he went to walk away, something shot past him and James watched as a stiletto met with the wall as Leila vented some of her fury towards the man who had walked out on her that morning. The man who had left her pregnant with his child.

'Were they any good, James?' Leila shouted. 'Did even one of them come close to us?'

James said nothing. He wrenched open the door and was met with security. 'Just in time,' James quipped. 'You can escort me down.'

He got back to his penthouse and paced, his mind racing.

'Well, well.' Muriel, his daily, who was

busy unpacking James's stuff from his trip to France, smiled.

'Well, well,' James said.

He liked Muriel. She was ancient and went about her business noisily, but was very possibly the one woman whose constant chatter didn't annoy him.

He flicked through his post that had gathered while he was away as Muriel chatted on.

'More money for me though,' Muriel said as she fixed him a coffee. 'Those sticky fingers…'

'It won't be living here.' James grinned.

'What, you won't bring *it* here on your access visits?' Muriel said, handing him coffee. 'Are you going to walk *it* around the park for a few hours once a week?' She gestured her head to the delicious view of Central Park. 'It would be a bit cold in winter.'

He hadn't thought that far; all he'd thought was that he didn't want Leila leaving the country.

'I'll see it when I visit Leila,' James said.

'Oh, my ex used to think he could just pop around whenever he wanted,' Muriel said. 'I soon put him right.'

'I bet you did.' James laughed, but when

Muriel had gone, he walked around his home, his absolute haven. A child? Here?

A baby!

He opened a spare bedroom that he was about to turn into a home theatre and he could not picture a baby in there, screaming its way through the night and wanting its mother.

He'd hire a nanny, James decided.

But Muriel had unsettled him. He was actually starting to think this through. By morning he had realised that she could leave at any moment, and with that thought he picked up the phone and was thankfully put straight through without The Harrington's usual games.

'I want you to move over to The Chatsfield,' James said. It was the only thing he could think of—at least that way he'd know if she checked out or if her family arrived to collect her.

'Why would I move there when I can stay here?'

'Leila,' James sighed. 'You can't afford to stay at The Harrington. And let me assure you Isabelle's charity will come at a price— she's not running a refuge for single moms.

Don't for a minute think her offer came from the goodness of her heart. She's doing this to dirty my family's name.'

'You manage that by yourself,' Leila responded. 'I'm not leaving here.'

'Leila, I'm not asking you to move into my home. I think this is an excellent idea. I'll have a suite arranged for you and I'll send a car to collect you at around lunchtime.'

'I have plans for lunchtime.'

God, she tested his patience to the limit. 'Tonight then,' James said, refusing to budge on this. 'I'll send my driver to collect you at eight.'

'I'm not moving out.'

'Will you at least agree to discuss it over dinner?'

'I don't want to have dinner with you. I don't want anything to do with you, James.'

'You should have thought about that three months ago,' James responded. 'Like it or not we have to communicate. I can call my lawyer and get discussions started or you can meet me tonight and we can try to work things out ourselves.'

'I will only meet with you in the restaurant.'

'Fine,' James reluctantly conceded. 'We'll

discuss our private business with half of the hotel watching on. Can you at least try and keep your shoes on this time?'

He ended the call and looked out to Central Park. The view sometimes soothed him but it didn't today.

She'd leave, in his bones he was sure of it, and there was not a thing he could do once she was gone.

He'd marry her, James decided, even if he'd run from the very idea all of his life.

As if she'd agree though, James admitted to himself. He could barely get Leila to agree to dinner without threatening her with a lawyer.

A sudden thought occurred and again he found himself on the phone to Manu, who was completely appalled at the idea he had just had and said that she would have no part in its execution.

'You can't force her to marry you, James, that's not fair.'

'She's pregnant with my child and could leave the country at any moment,' James clipped. 'I don't have time to be fair.'

CHAPTER SIX

LEILA *LOVED* MANHATTAN.

If she wasn't dreading meeting with James tonight, if she wasn't estranged from her family, if her heart wasn't lonely and heavy, then she would surely be singing as she dressed in the robe of gold she had arrived in before leaving the hotel to go to work.

Yes, work.

Leila had known she was in a holding pattern.

She had known that sooner or later the credit cards would stop, and she had decided that she would not be asking Zayn for money.

Yes, she was angry at him, yet she loved him.

He had asked her to trust him; he had promised that she would understand why Sophie had outed her and James if he could just explain.

She refused to let him.

Instead a very unskilled princess had attempted to get a job.

Rejected, disheartened, when her third trial at washing dishes had ended in its usual disaster, Leila had decided to cheer herself up by eating at her favourite Middle Eastern restaurant.

She had no idea it was incredibly exclusive. Leila simply ate the gorgeous food and enjoyed the gentle background music and then handed over the plastic at the end of her meal.

'Where is the music?' Leila had asked one day when the restaurant had only been filled with the noise of diners.

'We're trying to find someone,' Habib the waiter had said.

It turned out that they just had!

Now, each day from eleven till three, Leila played her beloved *qanun*. She had been shocked at first by the pittance they paid her, but was enjoying herself all the same.

Now the tips were growing and they had asked her to consider working at night, but Leila, too nervous to walk alone at night, had declined.

Leila worked through her shift and smiled when she saw her tips and then headed as she always did to Central Park.

Oh, she loved it there. She would walk around a lake or simply sit on a bench with her coffee. It was wonderful hearing the laughter and chatter as she sat there and pretended that she belonged.

'You're so young to have three children,' Leila said one day as a woman who looked like a teenager came and sat on the bench beside her and watched her children play.

'They're not mine.' The young woman smiled. 'I'm their nanny.'

'Nanny?' Leila checked.

'I look after the children while their mother works.'

'Oh!' Leila thought for a moment. 'Does she pay you to look after them?'

'Not very much,' the nanny grumbled.

She could do this, Leila decided as she walked back to the hotel. She could work and support her baby and she was going to tell James the same thing tonight.

He could carry on just as he had been, the louse.

The nannies all watched and sniggered as

a very beautiful woman in robes of gold let out a bellow of rage and kicked a tree.

Bastard!

She shouted it in her own language and would say it in his tonight when they met.

No way, no way did she like him anymore.

No way would she ever let him near her.

No way did she still want him.

And Leila reminded herself of that as she dressed to meet him that evening and chose a dress in red. She put on red sandals that were very high, but she chose them not for their colour, more because there were straps around the ankles so they might be difficult to take off when temptation hit.

She had fallen in love that night, and not only had he simply left her lying in bed, he had shamed her over and over after he'd left.

'We'll send someone to collect your luggage,' the receptionist said when she rang to inform Leila that Mr Chatsfield's driver was here.

'I'm not checking out,' Leila said.

She meant it. Leila would rather the embarrassment of a mounting unpaid debt than being kept by James.

Leila glanced at the magazine cover with

him and his tart on it simply to remind herself that the man she had met that night had been with others since then.

She imagined for a brief moment the future, explaining his salacious ways to their child.

She didn't even nod to the driver; instead Leila sat in the back of the limousine and decided to put some lipstick on.

For two reasons.

One, she remembered that he didn't like it on her.

Two, the name matched her mood, Leila told herself—she had pride.

'Why have we stopped?' Leila asked as the car came to a halt near Times Square.

'Mr Chatsfield's orders,' the driver said, and Leila followed his gaze. The square, always busy, had a large crowd gathering where the driver was looking and they were all pointing up at a sign and Leila looked up.

There were red hearts popping out but just as she went to read the words they disappeared and the image of a smiling James appeared. He was holding a ring and was down on one knee.

Leila felt sick.

The words were back now.

Marry me, Leila.

Never.

As simply as that, her decision was made and Leila went to get out of the car.

'Unlock this door,' Leila said to the driver, but he ignored her. 'You will unlock this door now,' Leila said, anger and panic mounting. 'That is a royal order.'

But instead of following her command, the divider slid closed and music came on instead.

No, she would not marry a man who had left her bed and jumped straight into another's. No way would she marry a man who only wanted her because she was pregnant. She had lived her life in a world without love and there was no way she would do that to either herself or her child.

Leila took a cleansing breath and tried to slow down her breathing. They would talk it through, Leila decided. There was no need for marriage; she had spoken with mothers at the park who raised their children alone.

They would come to the arrangements she had heard of.

Yes, she would speak to him, calmly, logically, and she would not throw a shoe this time.

Why was there a crowd outside The Chatsfield? Leila briefly wondered. Why were there photographers and people cheering as the door opened and she stepped out from the car?

Why was the red carpet covered in rose petals? And why was James walking out of the impressive entrance and making his smiling way towards her?

She wanted to turn and run but she could not, for to do so would publically reveal that it had been a one-night stand, not just to her people but later to their child.

It would insinuate she had been there only for sex.

Which she had been, Leila told herself.

No, that wasn't quite true, for she had been about to turn tail and run until she had seen James smile.

She stood on the carpet, trying to block out the shouts and cheers and the flashing lights of the cameras.

There was that smile she had fallen for, only she didn't welcome it tonight.

There was the man whom her body adored, for it wanted to run to him. Her shaking legs wanted to run to the shield of his arms, but her anger with him meant that she fought it as he walked towards her and finally came to a stand.

'Leila,' James said in a very clear voice. 'You are the only woman for me, I know that…'

She wanted to vomit.

For the past twelve weeks she had been brilliant at it, yet it wouldn't happen now.

She wanted to stand before the man who was holding out a ring and vomit at his feet. Yet her cover had been exposed and she was back to being a princess again, which meant she knew how to behave in public.

'You,' James continued his, for something that should surely be personal, rather loud speech, 'and our baby mean the world to me. I have never been happier than when I am with you. Like all couples we've had our ups and downs but I'm hoping,' James said, and then he hesitated and Leila frowned because she knew he was faking that he was possibly about to cry, 'in fact, I'm praying…' James dropped to his knees and held out a ring and she stood with poise.

Wait for it, James thought.

Just wait till that television crew was ready. Yep, now they were.

'Princess Leila of Surhaadi, and forever *my* princess, please give me the honour of making you my wife. Leila, will you marry me?'

She stared back at him, into his chocolate-brown eyes, and he was so bloody assured that he didn't even blink.

He knew as well as Leila did that she had no choice but to say yes.

'It would be *my* honour,' Leila suitably answered, and not just the crowd outside went wild. It was if the whole of Manhattan erupted, for in Times Square they had been holding their collective breath but started cheering when the news flashed up.

SHE SAID YES!

James placed the ring he had today chosen on her rigid finger and, as he stood, she gave him a loving smile. But her golden eyes flashed fire as he moved in to kiss her and then a smiling Leila moved her head.

'I hate you,' Leila whispered to his ear as their cheeks met the other's.

'I don't care.' James pulled back and smiled into her eyes and then sealed their fate with a very slow, very deep kiss, as the crowd sighed in pleasure.

It was done.

CHAPTER SEVEN

'YOU BIT ME...' James accused.

They were in the elevator, heading up to his suite, and James was wiping her lipstick from his mouth and trying to fathom that she had bitten his tongue, and worse, thanks to his gathered crowd, he hadn't been able to react.

'If you put your tongue in my mouth, then know it shall get bitten,' Leila said, tossing her hair in his face. 'Every time. And that wasn't a bite, that was a mere warning.'

They stepped off the elevator and walked hand in hand, smiling to the butler, who opened their door.

'Where's Leila's luggage?' James asked him.

'There was no luggage.' The butler responded in concern because James had been very specific with his instructions.

'I am keeping a room at The Harrington,' Leila sweetly explained.

'There's no need for that, darling.' James smiled to Leila and then spoke to the butler. 'Arrange for it to be brought over now, please, but don't bring it up till tomorrow. My fiancée is tired…'

'Your fiancée,' Leila said as the door closed on them, 'is furious. What the hell was that about, James? You forced me to say yes, you gave me no option but to say yes…'

'How many options did you give me?' James demanded. 'I had to find out via the media that I was going to be a father. You told your brother rather than me…'

'I told my brother because I didn't know what else to do and I wanted him to help me.'

'Well, he handled things brilliantly,' James sneered.

'I have already apologised for that,' Leila said. 'I wanted him to sort this out but…' She shook her head. 'I don't want that anymore. I know that I have to be responsible for my baby.'

'Well, guess what,' James shouted. *'So do I!'*

There was silence, just the sound of their

breathing, and then James told her how it would be.

'I'm not asking for the rest of your life, Leila. I don't want to be stuck in a loveless marriage any more than you do, but I *am* going to be there for my child. I'm not having him over for some bloody access visit, or worse, you taking the baby back to Sur… Sur…' He could think of nothing worse than a child in a country whose name he had only heard of yesterday, one he couldn't now pronounce.

'It's called Surhaadi!' Leila shouted. 'But now, thanks to you, I am not welcome there.' That wasn't strictly true, Leila knew. She hadn't been welcome in her home for twenty-four years, but she was too angry with James to stick to strict facts.

'Leila, your parents shall forgive you and when they do…'

'I was never intending to return there,' Leila said. 'I ran away, James, remember?'

'Well, I'm not taking that chance,' James said. 'I want seven years.'

'Seven?' Leila frowned. 'Why seven?'

'Give me the boy till he's seven…'

'It might be a girl.'

'I meant,' James gritted, 'that I want input during my child's formative years.'

He had thought about it. All night James had thought about the coldness of his own upbringing, the constant pressure. He wanted nothing like that for his child. He could barely stand the thought of his child knowing the pressure of being royal. Even if she didn't go back, what if she met someone else? He thought of how his father had been with his half-brother, Spencer, over the years, and no, James did not want some step-parent raising his own.

'We're going to do the right thing by this baby and the right thing is marriage.'

'There will be no sex in this marriage,' Leila hurriedly told him, sure that would put him off.

'Pity.' James shrugged. 'Because despite the terrible deflowering of precious maiden Leila, despite the fact your brother seems to think I forced you, that you were some poor little martyr lying there as big bad James coaxed you, the fact is you loved it, you wanted it and you pleaded for it.' He watched the colour burn on her cheeks. 'But you know what, Leila? Don't worry about sex—it's the furthest thing from my mind right now.'

He lied.

At the start of the sentence it had been, but recalling that night, even with bitterness, he wanted her again.

'Well,' Leila coolly responded, 'your behaviour in recent weeks means it is the furthest thing on my mind for the rest of my life, so know that before you take me as your bride.'

'We'll kiss for the cameras,' James said. 'We'll hold hands in public and we'll share a bed for the sake of the servants.'

'They are your servants,' Leila said. 'Surely you can pay for their silence.'

'Oh, my,' James laughed in her face. 'You know nothing about hourly rates, do you? Poor princess…'

She slapped him.

A little unmerited perhaps—he'd only called her by her title—but it felt so good. It felt better in fact than kicking a tree. She slapped him not just for that though, but for telling her he would shame her again by leaving her in seven years. For admitting that it would be a loveless marriage. It was the nightmare she had run from and she had no desire to live with a man void of feelings for her.

'If you weren't pregnant I'd slap you straight back,' James warned, and then he saw her gold eyes and acknowledged to her he lied. 'Actually, I wouldn't. It would seem that I come from slightly more modern stock than you.'

She went to slap him again but he caught her wrist.

'Savage lot the Al-Ahmars,' James said. 'But don't worry, dear Leila, because I'm not. You might not be familiar with them but I'm actually a gentleman.'

'You are no gentleman, James. Ask your *sharmotas*.'

Inexplicably he was almost smiling. Leila was like no one he had ever met, but instead of smiling James went and poured a very large drink of whisky and then went to pour her one but stopped. 'I guess you can't have one.'

'No,' Leila said, and her lips pursed when he took his drink and went to the bed. He kicked off his shoes and lay on top of the bed. 'I think that is rude,' Leila said. 'I can't have a drink and yet you do.'

'I do,' James said, and grinned as he took a sip. 'I'm not going to go on the wagon for the next six months.'

'So, you're just going to carry on as before…'

'And so the nagging starts.' James sighed and stretched out on the bed, propped up on one arm.

'Why did you bring me here and not to your home?' Leila asked. 'There we could have separate rooms.'

'We'll go there once we're married,' James said. His home was his haven and the thought of sharing it with anyone made him shudder, though he didn't tell Leila that. 'I think we might have slightly less chance of killing each other here. There's the restaurant, there's the gym, you can take yourself off for a spa, or whatever…'

'And it's public,' Leila said.

'Exactly.'

'James…' Leila took a breath. She didn't know how to tell him her truth but she made herself say it. 'I can't share a bedroom with you. I get bad dreams…'

'I'm having one at the moment,' came his glib response.

'I shout out,' Leila said. 'I cry.'

'You didn't the night…' His voice trailed off, for James did not want to think about that night.

'I forced myself to stay awake.'

'Do you grind your teeth?'

'I don't think so.'

'We'll go with the positives then.' He gave her a thin smile. 'So here we are.'

Here they were.

She looked at her finger marks on his cheeks. 'I am sorry I hit you.'

'Not that sorry,' James said. 'Given you went to again…' Then he saw tension in her features. 'It was a row.'

'Even so.'

'People row.'

She felt like crying. Leila had spent her life avoiding rows. She was just terrified of them and rightly so because the one row she'd had revealed her mother's truth.

'You don't have to force yourself to stay awake, Leila, and I'm not going to ship you off for a bit of noise. We all have our things. I'm sure, perfect though I am, there might even be a couple of things about me that annoy you…'

Oh, there were many things, but she chose

not to deal with the biggest one— that he had been with another since her.

'Like forcing me into a marriage I don't want?'

'Yep!'

'Like your socks?'

'Excuse me?' James frowned.

'They are horrible.'

'They're black socks,' James pointed out, but then he remembered her instruction to remove them, with so much authority to her voice that he'd thought she was about to produce a whip—they really knew anything about each other. 'You want me barefoot in robes, do you?' He peeled off his socks and threw them. 'Better?'

'It can never be better,' Leila said.

'How melodramatic.' James yawned.

'I'm going to have a bath.' It was the only place she could think of to get away from him.

She sat on the edge of the bath as it filled and thought about her situation. He seemed worried that she would flee, that her parents might come for her. He had no idea just how unwanted she was and was too embarrassed to tell him.

She would prove that he did not have to marry her, Leila decided. Over the coming weeks, she would show James that she could take care of herself and the baby.

She was surprised that he wanted to be in the baby's life. Leila honestly thought he would have been only too pleased to let her take care of things.

He surprised her at every turn.

Even as she came out of the bathroom dressed in a white fluffy robe, he did so.

He was undressed, his clothes were over a chair, but instead of getting into bed James was asleep on the long sofa with a blanket covering him.

'Thank you,' Leila said reluctantly, but he didn't stir.

Grateful for the reprieve Leila slipped into the vast bed and willed herself to stay awake.

James hadn't slept since he had found out he was going to be a father. Today had been exhausting—calling in all numbers of favours for the showy proposal. As soon as Leila had gone in the bathroom he had undressed and then set an alarm for six and had gone out like a light.

He didn't hear Leila come out of the bathroom and climb into bed. He didn't hear her stilted 'Thank you' for allowing her to sleep alone.

What he did hear a few hours later was the sound of agony.

James's eyes opened to the sound of her crying and it was the most pitiful sound that he had ever heard.

James had led a very privileged life, if void of much emotion. He had never heard pain like it. The tears were not loud, there was no shouting out, yet it was possibly the most wretched sound he had heard in his life.

He pulled a pillow over his head and tried to block out the sound, rather wishing that she *did* grind her teeth.

'Leila…' James went over to the bed, because he could no longer ignore it. He put his hand on her shoulder and tried to rouse her. 'You're dreaming.'

Still the crying continued and James lay on top of the bed and stroked Leila's shoulder. When she rolled into him, James wrapped his arm around her and the crying stopped.

He lay there in the city that never sleeps not sleeping just so that she might, wondering how best to explain why he was there in the morning.

Leila had never been comforted, not once.

No one had ever interrupted her tears, nor held her as she wept.

Apart from Jasmine's rare cuddles that always came at a price, no one had really held her at all.

It was alien, it was surreal, it was more beautiful than the feel of her silk gowns on her skin; it was more soothing than music.

Leila awoke to a naked chest on her cheek and James's arm around her. She hated him but would be forever grateful for knowing the balm of touch.

'Did I cry a lot?' Leila asked, mortified.

'You did,' James said. He could feel the heat of her blush on his chest. 'I kept saying, "It's fine, Leila, you're dreaming," and then I gave in and came to the bed. You will have observed that I didn't get in.'

'I did.'

He was about to say he was cold, or make some lame excuse to get under the covers, possibly for decency's sake because Leila was surely getting an eyeful as his morning erection attempted to escape the confines of his hipsters.

Leila actually hadn't noticed; she was willing the nausea to abate. God, it was bad enough that she'd been crying, but now here she was fleeing to the bathroom and there wasn't even time to close the door.

'You're quite a noisy housemate,' James said when she came out a little while later.

Leila smiled, embarrassed but grateful that he simply addressed things rather than ignored them. It was time for her to do the same because he had got into the bed.

'You're under the covers,' Leila accused.

'Because I've called for breakfast and I want the maids to see us looking all loving and happy,' James said, 'or will that make you feel sick again?'

She misunderstood.

'I feel better when I have eaten.'

'Does it happen a lot?' James asked, more curious than revolted.

'Most mornings. Earlier on it was any time of the day, but now it is just when I am hungry.'

She had brushed her teeth and rinsed her mouth and, a little pale, she sat on the sofa.

'I am sorry that you had to hear it though,' Leila said. 'Some things should be private.'

'Why?' James asked. 'I wouldn't worry about it—you're talking to the king of hangovers. Although I've given it some thought and I am going to go on the wagon.' He saw her frown. 'I've decided that I'm not going to drink while you can't. We'll crack open the champagne the day it's born.'

'That would be lovely.'

'Come to bed,' James said, and she startled.

'I would rather sit here.'

'Come here,' James said, and patted the bed beside him, but Leila shook her head.

'Well, sit on the sofa then.' James shrugged. 'But it's a bloody long way off. We'll have to keep saying "Pardon?" and "What did you say?" and it might look a bit odd to the maids.'

'Your English is too fast for me.'

'Come here,' James said. 'I can't say it any more simply than that.'

'No.' Still Leila chose the sofa. 'I don't care what your servants think of me.'

'Pardon?'

'I don't care what…' Leila started, and

then reluctantly smiled as she realised his little joke.

And James smiled back.

There was a knock at the door and James called for breakfast to be brought in.

Leila was very used to maids coming in in the morning. She asked for green tea sweetened with honey and for a pastry. James took his coffee and then told them they'd manage the rest but Leila called them back.

She told them to open the curtains and to run her a bath. She told them to add extra oils and to ensure that her luggage was here on the hour and could they get orange blossom honey for her tea in future.

'I bet you're popular with your servants back home,' James commented as one went to run the bath and the other left them alone.

'I was not.' Leila blinked.

'I was being sarcastic,' James said. 'You don't need to be so rude to them.'

'They are not your friends.' Leila knew that.

She knew how the servants whispered about the princess who even the queen did not want. It was servants who had removed her when she tried to speak to her mother.

Servants who had peeled a crying toddler from her mother's lap when she jumped on it and then scolded a little girl for upsetting the queen.

'It doesn't hurt to be nice,' James said.

'Sometimes it does.'

She could smell the fragrant bath water that was being run and it did not upset her stomach when so many scents did.

'I prefer the fragrances at The Chatsfield than the other hotel,' Leila admitted.

'Spencer will be very pleased to have your tick of approval,' James said, tucking into his second pastry, then he halted as she continued.

'I miss my scent,' Leila said.

So, too, did he.

'Every day,' Leila said, 'I think I have found it, every day I am disappoint.'

'Disappoint*ed*,' James mildly corrected her, and then he thought for a moment. 'Can you get it here?' he asked. 'I can have it made up if you tell me what the oils were.'

'I don't know what oils the maids used.'

The maid came out and said that her bath had been run and was there anything else Leila needed.

'You're dismissed,' Leila said, and then hesitated. 'Thank you.'

James watched her select a pastry.

'I thought you wanted a bath.'

'I bathe after breakfast," Leila said. 'I like to know it waits for me.'

"Well, I'm going to have a shower."

James headed for the shower as Leila nibbled her way through her breakfast.

The pastry was perfect, lovely and sweet, and the tea was refreshing and the honey here was actually quite nice.

When James came out of the shower he saw that the colour had come back to her face.

In fact, she was opening up a newspaper.

'I'd give them a miss if I were you,' James commented as he dressed.

'Why?'

'I just would.'

She unfurled the newspaper and was reminded why she was so cross with him when she saw the headline above a photo of them kissing just after James had proposed to her.

A Very Forgiving Princess.

'I'm not forgiving though,' Leila said to James, who was peering over her shoulder.

'Yes, well, my tongue had already worked that one out,' James said.

'Where are you going?' Leila asked as he headed for the door and, unused to such a question, James stiffened.

'We're not married yet, Leila,' James said, and continued towards the door, but he wasn't quick enough to get out before she delivered her warning.

'And if I have my way, we never will be.'

CHAPTER EIGHT

JAMES WASN'T PARTICULARLY looking forward to meeting with Spencer, but instead of the angry man who had spoken to him yesterday, Spencer was all smiles when James walked into his office.

In fact, Spencer stood and actually patted him on the back when James would far prefer that he didn't.

'Well done!'

'As I said, I thought the term used was *congratulations*.'

'I'm not talking about the baby.' Spencer grinned. 'Thanks to your little charade yesterday The Chatsfield is now *the* place to stay. Anyone who's anyone has got their PA ringing to make a reservation. We've got a certain royal couple coming over to New York to do some shopping. They've actually requested that the booking be changed from The Harrington to here! Isabelle will be spitting...'

James said nothing, or rather James said little throughout the meeting. He loathed the work side of things and did his best to avoid being at The Chatsfield unless it was for social reasons. It also irked him that everyone saw the baby as some sort of marketing opportunity, and Spencer naturally assumed that the wedding would be held here.

'We haven't even got around to discussing that.'

'Well, do,' Spencer said. 'A few more royal guests wouldn't go amiss. You could have a ceremony there if her parents wanted and then another one here...'

'Don't try and organise my wedding for me.' James stood. He could think of nothing worse than a Chatsfield wedding. 'We'll be going for something small and discreet.'

'It's a bit late for that,' Spencer said. 'Oh, and are you aware that Mommy Dearest has been trying to call you?'

'I am.'

'She thinks we should have a small dinner party in a couple of days to celebrate.'

James rolled his eyes. 'I'm busy.'

'Might as well get it over with,' Spencer said. 'You know what they're like. For appearances' sake they'll want it seen that you've taken your fiancée to meet them.'

'I couldn't give a rat's about appearances right now,' James interrupted. 'Isn't a public proposal enough?'

'If you are going to marry, then they'll have to all meet up sooner or later.'

James shuddered at the very thought, as he imagined Leila snapping her orders and his parents' response to the same. Still, with a sigh that Spencer recognised, he knew he'd have to face it.

'I'll tell them that you and your gorgeous fiancée will be there, shall I?'

James gave a very brief nod. 'I need to get back…'

'Are you worried she's going to abscond the moment your back's turned?'

'Her name is Leila,' James corrected, and then stalked out and headed back to the suite.

'Leila…' He knocked as he let himself in, but it soon became apparent that she wasn't there.

His heart galloped in his chest. Maybe Spencer's little dig about her absconding hadn't been such a remote possibility. He opened up the wardrobes and saw that all of her things had been delivered and put away. God, could Leila shop! There were clothes and shoes and bags and boots and when he walked in the bathroom there was a counter full of make-up and fragrances.

There must be a hundred of them!

There nearly was.

There was one for every day she had been here.

He understood her *disappoint* now as James remembered all the fragrances laid out on the table at her hotel and he thought of her in search of her own scent.

James walked back into the bedroom; the safe was open. Though he'd already guessed that if she couldn't operate the phone properly, then the safe might be beyond her. Finally he breathed again when he opened a drawer and found it stuffed full of cash and saw that her passport was there too.

Perhaps she'd decided to have a spa.

Or shopping perhaps, but no, he hadn't sorted out a credit card for her yet. James got on to that and as he was ordering one he pulled a curtain and looked down, worried about her out there alone and then telling himself she'd been here for three months now and had survived.

James then spent his requisite half hour updating his portfolio and was just about to take a very big gamble and move an awful lot of stocks into something not quite so secure, but with rapid potential indeed, when he hesitated. God, it had all been Monopoly money to him until now. All he had wanted to achieve was enough money to carry on living his depraved lifestyle and to leave his dysfunctional family behind.

He had much more than that on his mind now and it would seem that he might just have ended up with the most high-maintenance wife in the world! He chose a slightly more sensible option and just played the gamble with half.

And then he thought about Leila, searching for her own scent and the tears she had shed last night and he picked up the phone to fix the little he could.

She was a mystery.

A complete one because at 4:00 p.m. he looked up as the door opened and a very different-looking Leila walked in carrying several bags.

She was dressed in gold, and her long black hair was flowing; her eyes were made up with kohl. He had possibly never seen anything more beautiful but, just as relief hit, he also remembered how worried he'd been. 'Where have you been, Leila?'

'We're not married yet,' Leila said, and hit him with his own response to her question this morning.

'You look…' He was rather lost for words. 'Amazing.'

'Thank you,' Leila said. 'Though really I am so tired of wearing this robe but it is the only one I brought with me…' She was honest. 'I don't do well with the clothes here. I have tried so many things—I like to be covered but long dresses make me feel like a gypsy and trousers make me feel like a man.'

'You are so not a man, Leila.'

'I like being covered though.'

'I'll have someone come and bring a selection of clothes…'

'Authentic Surhaadi robes?' Leila shook her head. 'I think that might be a little hard for even James Chatsfield to arrange.' She opened up her handbag and took out a large wad of cash. 'Look at my tips.' Leila smiled.

'Tips?' James did a double take. 'Leila, where have you been?'

'Working.'

James blinked.

'So you were wrong yesterday—I do know about hourly rates!'

He couldn't believe that she'd gone and got a job.

'Where are you working?'

She told him where and James frowned; it was a very exclusive Middle Eastern restaurant close to where he lived, a restaurant that James visited on occasion. 'You're not waiting tables?' James checked.

'Of course not.'

'Dishes?' James asked in horror.

'Oh, no, I tried that three times and I got let go three times.'

'Belly dancer!'

She heard the hope in his voice and narrowed her eyes. 'Don't be crude,' Leila said, but she gave in to his curiosity, as it was incredibly nice to have someone who actually asked about her day and seemed interested. 'I play the *qanun* in the restaurant. They are delighted with me and have asked if I will do nights too.' She saw his mouth gape open. 'Did you think that I would have stayed hiding in my room, James?'

'I don't know,' he admitted.

'I earn little—one week would not pay for even one night here.'

'Er, it probably wouldn't get you an hour.'

'I get that, but it is the only job I could do. Now they are offering me more shifts for more money. It really is a start. I will not be a burden on you forever.'

'You don't need to work.'

'But I like it,' Leila said.

'I don't think you understand that you're known now.'

'I wear my veils to work,' Leila said. 'None of the customers know who I am. I like getting dressed up and playing my music. I like the appreciation. I like that I get a meal each day that I provide for.' She picked up some of the bags she'd brought in and took them over to the bar fridge and started to load it with containers of food. 'I like that I nourish my baby with food that I understand. James, I really do not need a husband. We don't need to get married...'

'Aside from everything, Leila, and it's just a minor point, but if you want to live here, then it might be preferable for you to be a US citizen and possibly the easiest way for you to get that is to marry me.'

'I don't understand.'

'You can't just *choose* which country you reside in. Don't take my word for it though, maybe check with the Surhaddi embassy.' James rolled his tongue in his cheek. 'If there is one.'

'I shall,' Leila snapped back. 'I mean it, James. I can support my baby. You are welcome to visit us when you wish but you don't have to fund me.'

She tested his patience but in a way that was starting to amuse him.

'So where *are* you going to live?'

'I will find somewhere.'

'On your music money?'

'Yes.'

'And what happens when the baby gets here?'

'I will still work. I will get a nanny.'

'On your music money?'

'Yes,' Leila answered, but then thought for a moment. 'Though you could maybe buy me a house.'

'And a couple of servants?' James checked, and Leila nodded.

'That would be very kind.'

'How about I try and see if there's a fiscal awareness course for displaced princesses?'

'How about you accept that despite your lavish proposal, despite your attempt to pressure me, it is not what I want. I don't want to be married to a man with a penis that acts like an untrained puppy jumping to greet any vague passerby.'

She looked at him and saw that he was smiling.

The oddest thing was, that even though she hadn't been joking, Leila found herself smiling back.

'Was that a row?' Leila checked.

'It was a discussion,' James said. 'Now, I've found an OB—you have an appointment tomorrow, at six.'

'Six?' Leila checked. 'But I eat my dinner at six.'

'She's staying back to accommodate you.' James rolled his eyes at her ingratitude. 'I've also booked dinner in the restaurant tonight for seven but I can change it to six if you prefer.'

She wrinkled her nose.

'What?' James asked. 'What's wrong with that?'

'Your array of silverware tires me,' Leila said, and then flounced off to bed for a rest as she often did in her life, simply to pass time.

She was very used to a knock on the door that woke her in the evening and told her she was allowed to come out for dinner.

Leila sighed as James gently knocked and reminded her that dinner awaited. She rolled from the bed and padded out to get a glass of water before she dressed up for dinner and then she froze.

The lights were dim; there was cloth on the floor and cushions too. The food she had brought back from the restaurant was dressed on beautiful plates and there was a package of silver in the middle with a bow.

'I thought that we might eat here,' James said as she sat down. 'Not a fork in sight.'

He poured her some lovely cool tea and she sipped it. As she tore some pita and ladled it with minted lamb, her eyes were drawn to the silver box, but she did not comment.

'Why are we not eating in the restaurant?'

'Because…' James shrugged and then

looked over to her. 'I didn't think you'd prefer to eat here. Most people like eating out.'

'I do,' Leila said. 'I was very excited to try it when I first came here, but I find it all just so confusing. I like the restaurant that I work at. I recognise the food there.'

'I might have to pay it a visit again,' James said. 'I hear they have an amazing musician.'

He got the reward of a small smile.

'Don't tell me if you ever come in,' Leila said. 'It might make me nervous to play.'

'Well, you'll see me if I do,' James said, but Leila shook her head.

'I don't lift my eyes to meet the guests.'

The food was amazing, even by James's high standards, and yes, he might drop in for dinner one night to hear her play.

'Maybe it would be nice to eat out more,' Leila mused as she thought of going out to dinner with James and the nice way he explained things to her. She didn't tell him that part though. 'Now that I don't feel so unwell.'

'How long have you felt unwell?'

'Pretty much since the morning you left.' Her voice was accusing and she looked at him and then acknowledged to herself that those early days after he had so coldly left her had been grief. She had lain on her bed crying and shut herself away just to mourn the man who had walked out on her. 'Well, a couple of weeks after you left me alone after a whole night of making love to me…' She watched the press of his lips as she remade her point. 'Then the ill feeling started. I had no idea what was wrong.' She blinked and he could see her confusion as to that time.

'Tell me,' James said, because he had missed out on so much. 'When did you know you were pregnant?'

'Not for a few weeks. I was ill and thought it was because of the different food, but even when I stopped eating it and went to a restaurant where the food was more familiar, still I felt sick. I asked the hotel to send me honey water but it tasted wrong. In my home the honey is from bees that pollinate orange blossom. I have a very sensitive palate… I told them to call for a doctor when I could not even keep honey water down. She came to the room and…' Leila could still recall the shock, from being told to pass urine onto a plastic stick of all things, to being told that she was with child. 'I told her I was on the pill.

'I tried calling you and then when Zayn tracked me down I had to tell him what was wrong.' She was a little bit more giving with information. 'My sister, Jasmine, was in trouble with men when she died. That is why my brother is so protective of me,' Leila lightly explained. 'When I told him you left after one night and didn't come back, that you didn't even call…'

'It was supposed to be a one-night stand.'

'Well, it didn't feel like it,' Leila said, and she stared at him. For the first time she saw colour darken his cheeks and he shifted in discomfort, for no, it had not felt like a one-night stand at the time.

'How do you do it, James?' Leila challenged. 'How do you kiss with such passion and make love to a body and then walk away?'

'Leila, I sent you flowers not once but five times and still you didn't pick up the phone. Do you really think I was going to stay celibate just in case ten years from now you might suddenly decide that you'd changed your mind?'

'You sent me flowers?' Leila frowned.

'You didn't get them?' James checked, furious at the florist and about to declare that heads would roll when Leila spoke.

'The floral displays that were delivered to my room were all from you?'

'Hello!' James said. 'Did you not read the cards?'

'What cards?' Leila said.

'The card that came with the flowers? Didn't you read them? Did you even notice them?'

'The flowers at the palace get changed every day. I thought it was that. I told them off for not taking the old ones out.' She was still frowning. 'Why would you send me flowers?'

'To thank you for that night, to ask you to dinner, to ask you to please just pick up the phone…'

'I rang the number three and complained when the floral displays stopped arriving,' Leila said, and was surprised by the sound of his laughter.

Not just surprised that he was laughing, but surprised at how much she had missed it and how that very sound made her lips want to smile.

She did not let them though; instead they pursed because she was so very hurt by him.

'When the flowers clearly weren't working I went to France.' James explained a little of what had been happening to him. 'I went there in an attempt to get you out of my head. It didn't work. I came back a couple of weeks ago and, sad bastard that I am, was heading to The Harrington hoping to see you when I ran into your brother—after that I decided to head back to France till the dust had settled and only then...' He didn't elaborate.

He didn't need to.

It was a regrettable fact for both what had occurred from that point on.

'Why don't you try speaking with your brother?'

'I miss my brother,' Leila said. 'But I am cross with him.'

'What about your parents?' James pushed. 'Surely the fact we are getting married must help.'

'I doubt it. I just hope that, though they won't forgive me, they don't hate my baby,' Leila said. 'I want them to love my child and not take it out on him or her.'

Which, to James, seemed a rather reasonable request.

They carried on eating and when her eyes lingered again on the present, James moved it towards her.

'Are you going to open it?' James asked, for he was as impatient as she was.

'What is it?'

'A present.'

'For?' Leila checked, for she was used to her mother and to Jasmine getting presents. She had been gifted stones from other palaces although she did not dare get her hopes up that this might be a present for her.

'You.'

She had never had a personal present before. Especially not one that was wrapped in pretty paper and had a bow that took forever to open.

'Come on, Leila,' James said, but not with the snarky impatience he had used the day she had taken forever to dress.

'What is it?' Leila asked, and opened a box and stared at a small dark bottle.

'Open it.'

She unscrewed the small lid and bent her

head and James watched as she closed her eyes and inhaled her scent.

'It's me,' Leila said, and poured some oil on her fingers. 'But how?'

'I'm not telling you,' James said, and watched as she ran her fingers through her hair and added a drop to her throat.

She smelled now of that night and it was a dangerous place to recall. Especially when James later said goodnight and stretched out on the sofa. But the glitter of tears in her eyes when she'd opened it had made it worthwhile.

Leila stared at the ceiling. 'Thank you,' she said, and this time he heard it.

'You're welcome.'

'Why did you buy me a present?'

'Why not?' James asked.

'But why?' Leila persisted.

'I hate that you're homesick.'

She wasn't though. Leila stared into the dark and tried to recall a night when she had known such care of her heart, even if it came from a man who didn't love her.

When later she cried, James walked over and shook her shoulder, and when still she cried, instead of lying on top of the bed this time he got in. Leila rolled into him and he inhaled the delicious scent of her. He'd had his shirt, the one that held her fragrance from their one night together, analysed. Now a scent with a base of jasmine and a woody note of oud, frankincense and musk lingered in delicate combination, and James drew her closer in.

Oh!

Leila lay with his heartbeat in her ear and strong arms around her and lovely hairy legs beneath her smooth ones and a hand that caressed her arm. She awoke to it too, and lingered there just a moment, trying to pretend she was still asleep, just to revel in the feel of another. The crinkle of hair on his stomach had her fingers itching to explore but she denied them.

'You got in,' Leila said as she untangled herself and lay on her back on a sheet that felt too cool.

'You didn't complain when I did.' James looked over and smiled. 'You were purring like a cat.'

Leila poked out her tongue to him and then got back to staring at the ceiling.

'I don't feel sick.'

'Yay!'

'Do you think that could be bad?'

'Of course not, you're a textbook pregnancy. Well, according to Dr Internet—morning sickness fades in the second trimester.'

'You looked it up.'

'Of course I did.'

She liked that he did.

'You can ask the physician all your questions this evening,' James suggested. 'I know what I want to ask her…'

'You?' Leila frowned. 'I don't want you there.'

'Well, I have to be there,' James answered tartly, and got out of bed.

'Where are you going?' Leila asked.

'To the shower,' James said.

'But breakfast will soon be delivered,' Leila protested because she was enjoying speaking with him.

'I'm over impressing the maids too,' James responded.

'You're cross.'

'Yep.'

'Because?'

'I'm sure you shan't bother to work it out.'

They barely spoke all morning and it was

a relief when Leila went to work. James rang Manu to ask about a dressmaker for Leila but was taken aback when Manu responded angrily.

'Did you speak with her family before you proposed to her?' Manu asked. 'Have you included them in your plans?'

'No.'

'That is offensive,' Manu said.

'I'm trying to do the right thing here,' James said. 'I asked her to marry me, didn't I? Surely that's the right thing to do by them?'

'James, she is a princess, her father is a king…'

'Well, what the hell was I supposed to do?'

'Not railroad her into marrying you. Not cause irreparable damage between her and her parents might have been a good start. You should have listened to me when I told you not to do this.'

'Just give me the name of a dressmaker,' James snapped, irritated, yet Manu's words had rattled him. And they were still niggling even as they sat at the doctor's and he filled out five hundred forms that made even him blink.

He was rather tempted to ask if her harp

money might fund an overseas visitor to the US for a pregnancy but decided to choose his battles wisely.

And he chose not to say anything when the receptionist called her name and Leila stood.

'Did you want James to come in?' the receptionist offered. 'Catherine will be doing an ultrasound.'

'I'll be fine,' Leila said. 'You may not believe it but I'm actually quite capable.'

God, she was arrogant, James thought as Leila strode in.

Leila wasn't just arrogant, she was terrified.

She did not want to be examined, and neither did she like all the questions that Catherine asked. However, when she lay there trying to be brave as Catherine put some jelly on her stomach, Leila *did* work out why James had been cross this morning.

Only then did she understand why James might have wanted to be here because there on the screen was their *baby*. This tiny little thing with a tiny head, arms, legs, fingers, hands and a nose. It even kicked its little legs and Leila was almost overcome with emotion as she saw what that night had made.

'We'll do a more thorough ultrasound at eighteen weeks but for now everything looks completely fine. Do you have any questions?'

Leila shook her head.

Catherine tried to engage her, tried to get more information from her, but Leila refused to go there. As she stepped out of the examination room there was James waiting and she could see the anxiety on his features.

'It is the size of a pea pod,' Leila said, and held up her thumb and finger in a guess of the size. 'It has a nose.'

'That's good to know,' James said, and she handed him a photo.

'If you want to, there is another ultrasound in about five weeks' time. I think you might like to see it.'

'I'd like that a lot,' James said.

'Where I come from a man would not be there for such a thing. I thought you were offering to come in with me out of sympathy…'

James gave her a smile as they worked a little more of the other issues out. 'Dinner?' he asked.

Leila nodded.

Choosing to walk, James dismissed his

driver and they went to a gorgeous Italian restaurant that was tucked away from the busy crowds. It was so nice to sit and relax and simply talk and eat as they both took turns to look at the ultrasound photo and admire a very beautiful nose.

'Are you going to find out?' James asked.

'Find out what?'

'If you're having a boy or girl.'

'Does it matter?' Leila asked, and her voice held a challenge.

'Of course not.'

'It did in my family,' Leila said. 'My parents hoped I would be a boy.'

'Well, I'm very glad that you're not,' James said, and when she didn't return his smile he knew there was a much bigger hurt there. He could never have fathomed just how much. 'I am sorry for the trouble with your family.'

'It is not your fault.'

'I'm quite sure that your parents don't agree,' James said. 'Do you miss them?'

He watched her struggle to respond. Leila truly didn't know how to answer him, for yes, she missed them but she had missed them all her life.

'Maybe once the baby is here they'll come around?' James gently suggested, but she gave a small shake of her head and he could see that she was struggling so he left it.

For now.

'I got you this…' James went into his pocket.

'Another present?' Leila excitedly asked, and then pouted when he gave her a phone. 'So you can track me.'

'You can track me too.'

'I don't know how to use it,' Leila admitted.

'It's all set up for you.' James pulled out his and her phone bleeped and Leila looked to the screen that said *James.*

He was very patient and walked her through it and she smiled when she saw the text he had sent.

We make beautiful babies.

It was a very nice first text to have from him and it took a few goes but finally Leila replied to him.

We do.

Dinner was served and Leila discovered that she loved pasta and was delighted at a new use for her fork as she twirled spaghetti around it, like James did, pressing it into the spoon.

'It tastes so good!' Leila said. 'Just so creamy and fantastic!'

'And it comes in so many shapes and sizes too!'

His sarcasm was completely wasted on Leila; she just smiled. 'Does it? I can't wait to try them all.'

'Well, while I've got you in such a good mood, I have two things to tell you. Do you want the good news first or the bad news?' James offered.

'The bad news,' his back-to-front fiancée replied.

'We have to go to dinner with my parents tomorrow night.' He pulled a face. 'Spencer will be there too. It will be awkward and un-comfortable and I just want to tell you up front that any tension has nothing to do with you—in public they're fine, in private it's a subdued hell.'

'You really don't like them!'

'I really, really don't,' James said, and he

chose to explain the strange dynamics to her. 'My father, Michael, isn't the sunniest person. They married young and my father, just like his brother, cheated…'

'At what?' Leila asked.

'He cheated on my mother,' James explained. 'He had affairs, rather a lot of them. Anyway, he was always a bastard growing up, especially to Spencer, and recently we found out why. Well, *I* found out why. My other brother Ben found out when he was eighteen and it turns out that was the reason he left home…'

'Found out what?'

'That my mother had an affair of her own, and it turns out that Spencer isn't my father's…'

'Your mother cheated too!'

'She did!' James matched her wide eyes. 'You are so completely shockable.'

'But it *is* shocking. Does your father know?'

'Yep. There was a massive row a few years back and it all came out. He'd always guessed, which is why he was even meaner to Spencer. No one mentions it now though.'

'They just carry on as normal?'

'Hardly normal,' James said. 'You'll see it for yourself soon. Anyway, I'm very sorry to inflict them on you.'

'It's fine.' Leila shrugged. 'What is the good news?'

'I've found you a dressmaker,' James said. 'I've asked her to come tomorrow afternoon. You shall have new robes...'

'And slippers?'

'And slippers,' James said.

He had found more than a dressmaker. On Monday he was starting Arabic lessons. Whatever James put his mind to he succeeded at, and he had no doubt, after intensive private lessons that, in a few weeks' time, he would be able to speak with her father and explain the little that Leila wanted—for them not to take their anger with him and Leila out on their child. Not that he told Leila that. His father had been so demanding, so critical, that James never revealed anything till it was achieved.

It was a cool evening but they again chose to walk, and was it for potential cameras that they held hands?

Leila wasn't sure; she just knew that she liked it.

And she wasn't sure if the hand that went around her waist when they passed a rowdy group standing on a corner was for her sake, or the sake of the baby.

They walked towards The Chatsfield and just a little way away from it James stopped and turned her around.

'A kiss for the cameras?'

'Where are they?'

'Oh, the press are always sniffing around The Chatsfield. There's always some scandal going on.'

'One kiss then,' Leila agreed.

One blissful kiss that was light and delicious. His lips were warm and they teased, and when he pulled her a little into him, his hand was back on her waist. He hadn't shaved since the proposal and she liked the roughness of his jaw and remembered how it had felt on her mouth that night.

He stepped in a fraction closer and she wanted his coat around them; she remembered how they had danced. Leila remembered how those lips, how that rough jaw, had felt when he had kissed her some place other than her mouth and her lips parted.

She wanted more passion, she wanted a more intimate taste of him, and she opened her eyes to find his were open too, smiling into hers as he refused her his tongue.

'Once bitten...' James said, pulling away, very, very pleased as to how much she had liked it.

Oh, she had.

She was blushing in the elevator as she remembered the kiss he had given her in here. She didn't know that the tune he was whistling was 'Memories'; she just knew she was under a different but delicious attack by his mouth.

They headed up to their suite and when Leila came out from taking her make-up off James was in bed.

'If I go to the sofa I'm staying there for the whole night,' James warned, and he knew that he'd won because she shrugged and came over to the bed and climbed in.

'You've got a bump,' James commented, because he had noticed the little swell of her stomach as she came out of the bathroom.

'I know!'

She picked up her little bottle of oil and rubbed some into her hands and then smelled them.

'Will you buy our baby such nice presents?' Leila asked.

'I already bought it one when I got your ring.'

'Really?' Leila said, and then examined the ring that she hadn't so much as glanced at when he had put it on.

'It's actually very beautiful,' Leila admitted. It was. A platinum band was beaded with little diamonds but it was the huge centre stone that Leila was examining, and she sat up in bed watching it sparkle under the light. 'Who gifted the stone?'

James smiled at her odd question. 'Tiffany's.'

'I can't believe that it fits.'

James could.

As he watched her long slender fingers he recalled buying the ring. The jeweller had said it could be sized later. And yet, he had pictured her fingers so many times. Pictured them tracing his body and he had also suckled each one with his lips. He had placed the jeweller's sizer on the very tip of his little finger and had known beyond doubt that the ring would fit.

Leila turned out the light. James had remembered just a little too much of that night and the kiss downstairs had only confirmed their attraction and so he reached for her.

Leila fought with herself as she lay there on her side with her back to him. His hand was on her stomach and she could feel the heat of his palm as he stroked her newly emerged bump.

He held her most mornings but that was when she went to him.

This was different from that, Leila knew.

She was angry at the want in herself, at the temptation to turn around to his mouth as he started to kiss her shoulder and move his lips up to her neck. She was angry because as his hand stroked her stomach she was willing it to move down.

It obliged.

And still she lay there, fighting herself, for she wanted the roam of his hand and Leila wanted the skill of his mouth. She didn't want to be in want of him; she didn't want the power of his touch to enslave her again. She didn't want the weakness that his touch and words procured, for he was telling her now that he was crazy about her, that he craved her scent, her skin.

He turned her towards him and he came half over her, his mouth seeking hers, his erection nudging against her thigh, and the weight of him was blissful. She ached for his kiss, yet she refused it; she would not give all of herself to him. Leila moved her head so that when she spoke it was to his cheek.

'Just do it.'

'Excuse me?'

'You don't have to kiss me, you don't have to caress me, you don't have to tell me you care—just do it...'

'Can you feel that?' James asked, and didn't wait for her answer. 'I doubt it, because it isn't there any more.'

She got then that he was talking about his erection, or what had been one.

He cussed and then turned on his back and they lay in tense silence until Leila broke it.

'Is it me you want?' Leila checked. 'Or is it just that I am here.'

James rolled his eyes. 'Oh, it's you.' He looked over. 'You'd be a pretty hard fantasy to top.'

She turned her back to him.

'Look what happened when I wasn't here.'

'Yes, I do get what you're saying,' James conceded. 'We're forced together, but that doesn't mean...'

'*You* forced us together, James,' Leila interrupted. 'You pushed for this just because you want to be close to the baby, so that I couldn't take him or her with me. So please don't rewrite history and don't try to pretend that you gave me a choice.'

'Why don't *we* rewrite our history?' James nudged. 'Why don't we start being nice to each other and try dating—holding hands...' He yawned. 'Conversation. All the stuff that I've spent my life avoiding.'

'Why?'

'Because I'm hot for you, Leila,' James said, and he made her cheeks pink. 'Because I remember how good we were and it's going to be a bloody long seven years otherwise.'

'James...' She turned and looked at him, at her very honest playboy, and she offered a suggestion. 'It isn't a turn-on when you keep pointing out we have a limited time frame.'

'Noted.' James smiled at the progress they made. 'I'm going to date you, Leila.'

He watched as she tried to hold on to a very reluctant smile. 'And given I can't wine you, I'm going to have to dine you. A lot. After tomorrow though.'

'After tomorrow?' Leila checked.

He let out a sigh. 'We're having dinner with my parents, remember?'

CHAPTER NINE

LEILA WAS MEASURED for her new robes and slippers. It went on for the entire afternoon. She chose from swatches of heavy silks in light colours and made her selection of beads and threads. It was so different from home where her clothes simply arrived and Leila was expected to wear them without comment.

'They're going to be beautiful,' Leila said as she told James about them when he came out of the shower to dress for dinner with his parents. 'I have chosen soft colours— back at home it was all silver and gold...' She could sense his distraction and her voice trailed off. 'What should I wear to meet your parents?'

'Whatever you feel most comfortable in,' came James's less than helpful response.

She could feel his tension and she recognised it, for it was how Leila had felt every day when she had lived at the palace.

Leila selected her gold robe and she did up the little buttons at the back that her maid had usually done. James tried *not* to watch the small struggle it took for her to do that. He tried *not* to remember the night she had unzipped her dress for him while, at the same time, Leila sulked that he did not help her.

'Did you get buttons at the front for your new robes?' James asked once Leila had finally done them up.

'A woman of standing has buttons at the back and doesn't do up her own. It is *common* to have them at the front.'

She noticed him, too, though.

There were beads of water on his back that he had missed while drying. As he went to get out his shirt, Leila wanted to take up the towel and dry his back. She wanted to kiss his tense shoulders, but instead she watched as he slipped his shirt on and selected a tie.

'You didn't shave,' Leila commented because he had said that he was going to.

'And I didn't cut my hair,' James clipped, and then he saw her frown. 'You'll see.'

They were driven to his parents and Leila attempted conversation. 'I am thinking that maybe I should try and ring my parents,' Leila said. 'Though no doubt I have been disowned.'

'I dream of the day my parents disown me…' James stared moodily out of the car window and then stopped. 'That was insensitive.'

'You are at times.' Leila turned and smiled. 'I like that about you.'

'Like what?'

'That you speak your truth.'

'Well, you're the only one who does!'

He took her phone and she gave him the number of the palace phone and he found the international code for Surhaadi, which he tapped into the phone.

'It's there when you're ready to call them.'

'It rings in their lounge,' Leila said, and she closed her eyes remembering the last time she was there. She knew she might never be brave enough to ring them.

It helped to know that she could though.

'Come on then,' he said as they arrived at his parents' home. God, he remembered the misery of coming home on school holidays…

James was certain it was going to be a miserable night.

James took her hand and they walked from the car to his parents' door.

As they stepped inside and he introduced Leila, James was aware again of her incredible poise and beauty and he was aware, too, of the pride in his voice as he introduced her.

'This is my fiancée, Leila.' He watched as her father offered his hand and he saw she was a touch tentative taking it but Leila did.

'This is my mother, Emily.'

'It's lovely to meet you,' Leila said, and though Emily nodded she didn't offer her hand, she was too busily clinging to her wine glass.

'This is my brother Spencer.'

Spencer offered his hand and Leila tapped her heart.

'That means she doesn't want to shake your hand, Spencer.' James grinned, quite sure that it was for the very last time that night.

It wasn't.

'Nice of you to shave,' Michael said to his son as they took a seat in the lounge.

'It's a family dinner,' James pointed out,

and declined his usual whisky and asked for sparkling water and a slice of lime instead.

Leila watched as Michael raised his eyes and James let out a breath. 'Don't worry, Father, just because I've asked for water it doesn't mean that I'm gay.' He glanced over to Leila. 'Real men drink whisky apparently.'

His father's criticism towards James was as constant as it was relentless and it felt a lot like home to Leila. She gave James a tiny wink when his father called him Jiminy and it caught James by surprise and he gave her a little wink back.

Nothing could really ease it though.

'You could at least get your hair cut,' Michael said, and smacked James upside the head in a gesture that was surely designed purely to humiliate as James took a seat at the dinner table. 'You're in the press a lot of late.'

'I don't dress for the tabloids.'

'No, it would seem that you *undress* for them.'

James shot his father a warning look that went ignored.

'Well,' Michael graciously conceded, as he rudely referred to Leila's pregnancy, 'at least you've dealt well with the current mess you've found yourself in. It's good to see that you're doing the respectable thing by the Chatsfield name for once.'

This time James didn't warn him with his eyes. He didn't like his father speaking like that in front of Leila—and pointing out that they were getting married for the sake of the pregnancy was one step too far, though of course they were.

Leila surely didn't need it rammed down her throat and so James challenged him. 'Don't think for a moment that Leila and I are marrying for the sake of the Chatsfield name.'

'I'm just saying it's good that for once you're behaving.'

'I always behaved. I was the perfect son for eighteen years...'

'And then an absolute disgrace for the next decade.'

'Ah, but it was fun,' James said, taking a slug of sparkling water and wondering what the hell had possessed him to give up booze for the next six months.

They limped through dinner with only one highlight.

Leila did mind her manners with his parents, but James suppressed a smile when she called one of the maids over and told her to re-serve her meal but this time without meat.

'Is she a vegetarian?' Emily frowned. 'James, you could have at least warned us.'

'No, I'm not a vegetarian,' Leila said. 'It's not James's fault—I just don't like the way the cook prepared the meat tonight.'

Yes, he grinned, but as he sat at the table and James saw the zoned-out expression of his mother as she topped up her wine glass, he thought of Leila, forced to be with someone she didn't want to be with. He loathed the absolute charade that his parents' marriage was and all because neither had the guts to get out.

Leila had the guts.

Was he forcing her into this?

No, James decided as dessert was served. For he respected Leila and cared for her and he was doing this for the sake of their child.

Still, a night with his family meant that any seeds of doubt as to what he was doing to Leila got a very thorough soaking.

He wanted out of there; he wanted back to his sham of a relationship with Leila because it felt a lot better than his parents' home.

Even before his hastily drained coffee cup had hit the china saucer James was standing.

'We're going to go.'

'Already...'

'Leila gets tired,' James said.

'Don't use me as an excuse again,' Leila warned as they drove back to the hotel, but James ignored her and so she said it again when they were back in their suite.

'I said, don't use me or the baby as an excuse, just because your father is a vile...'

'Oh, please,' James interrupted, 'surely there has to be at least one perk to having a pregnant fiancée, and if it means I get out of dinner with my family early, I'm going to use it.'

'Oh, so that's the only perk, is it?'

'Well, it's certainly not...' James stopped but not in time, and Leila soon worked out what he'd been about to say.

'So much for dating me,' Leila said. 'So much for taking our time.'

She huffed off to the bathroom and removed her make-up and when she came out James had undressed and was in bed.

She pulled back the sheet and climbed in and lay there bristling.

'Sorry about that,' James said. 'They just bring out the bastard in me.'

'I get it,' Leila said, because her own family didn't exactly bring out the princess in her.

She really did get it.

Leila thought back to the night when everything had come to a head, how she'd run to a foreign land.

To him.

He pulled her into his arms and she lay there. He kissed the top of her head and Leila couldn't tell him that she'd never been happier in her life. That she'd never been sadder too. That she'd never felt more than she did right now.

'Are they always so critical?' Leila asked.

'Always,' James said. 'That's actually them on a good day.'

'Your mother doesn't say much,' Leila commented.

'When would she get a chance? I want away from them, Leila, but I keep getting dragged back in.' James closed his eyes but not to go to sleep. They were all nagging for it to be a Chatsfield wedding, given that James had made it such a public proposal.

The most annoying part for James as he

lay there was that he'd dragged himself back into it this time.

For one reason.

Make that two.

She felt his tension also and she wanted it gone. She remembered her own and how he had soothed hers away that one night. She was truly scared though to give that part of herself to him again. To call his name out, to admit to loving him, which she had come to realise she truly did. Despite herself.

He already had her heart forever.

Leila would just prefer for him not to know it.

She could never forget what he had done for her though, and Leila wanted to do something for him.

Leila remembered removing the condom and kissing him intimately, and how it had driven him right to the edge and then he'd taken her.

She could do that without giving him her love.

'Er, Leila…' James said as her hand moved down his stomach and then she felt him beneath her fingers.

He felt like the red velvet panties, as soft

and as forbidden as they were. Yet, this was alive and it grew to her touch. She started to kiss down his chest as her head moved down his stomach and James lay there frowning. 'Leila, you're not asleep, are you?'

'No,' Leila laughed, and he felt her breath and it stirred him.

'You're not having a rude dream that I'm going to have to somehow explain in the morning?' James checked, and she laughed again as she shook her head and started to kiss the softest skin.

Leila liked how he grew; she liked, too, that when she took to her knees, his hand sought to touch her but she removed it. She licked him as she had that night until he was hard and aching for more pressure. He had to have been, for when her lips went over him and she took him in, he moaned at the temporary relief her mouth gave. Temporary because the hand on her head urged her to take him deeper and then with brief apology he removed it.

Leila reached for his hand and led it back to her head, not just because she liked the guidance but it was safer there, for she wanted him to touch her too.

It had been for him, yet it was turning her on in a way she chose to deny.

Her face was as hot as her sex as his thighs tensed with the effort of not thrusting.

She used her mouth more, she used her tongue more, she used her mind more because she wanted to move her hips. Leila wanted her sex on his face and as James suddenly swelled she recognised that he was close to the time when he had come inside her; the memory was enough for Leila. As tension peaked and then started to leave him, Leila came too. As she tasted and swallowed and then tasted some more she denied though that she was. Even as she sat back on her heels and swallowed the last of him down, she denied the pleasure between her own legs that was still flickering and told herself that it had been only for him.

'It was a one-off,' Leila warned as she went back to his arms. 'For dealing with your family.'

It was the third time James grinned that night. 'Shall I ring them now and tell them we'll be there for breakfast?'

She rather hoped that he might.

CHAPTER TEN

JAMES, WHO HAD always hated spring, simply because it meant the end of the skiing season, started to sink into this one. He enjoyed the laughter, and evenings spent getting to know Leila better.

The money in Leila's drawer grew and grew and the restaurant where she still worked had an undercover princess that was proving a sensation on her own.

She seemed happy by day, but James loathed her tears at night. He had decided that he would do what he could to resolve things, but Arabic, James soon found out, was a spectacularly hard language to learn.

Even with a very experienced teacher.

Day after day he sat in a small office with smaller windows and, even three weeks into his lessons, James had barely got past the alphabet and a few small phrases. 'You were never going to be fluent in a matter of weeks.' Nadir, his coach, merely smiled at his frustration late one Friday afternoon.

'I was good at languages at school,' James said. 'I just don't feel that I'm getting anywhere.'

'You shall if you persist,' Nadir said. 'Now, I am away next week, but I have given you plenty to work on. Could you perhaps try speaking in Arabic with Leila?'

James shook his head. He was trying to prove his competence, not his idiocy. He had fast learned to school himself in private. He remembered the disapproval of his father—every Christmas card, every birthday card he had written had earned him hours more homework for poor handwriting. It had been the same with French and the same again with Latin. Michael Chatsfield seemed to believe that children should be born fully trilingual and with a healthy understanding of applied mathematics.

'Your hair's nice,' James said as he came into their suite.

She had had it curled and it was loosely pinned up and though she was wearing a towel all her make-up was on. They were going out tonight and could not be late, though he hadn't told Leila where he was taking her.

'Busy day?' Leila asked.

'Frustrating,' James said as he rapidly undressed for the shower.

She wondered when he said *frustrating* if he was referring again to the lack of sex, because since that night there had been nothing.

By her choice.

Though James to his credit had not pushed her.

Perhaps she knew why?

Leila loathed how he quickly stripped, and was starting to think that the fact he came home each night smelling of some other's perfume was the reason.

She expected no less—a quintessential playboy forced into marriage who, by his own admission, came from a family of cheats.

James jumped in surprise when she walked into the bathroom where he was showering and saw that she had her angry-camel face on. 'What?' he asked.

Had the maids left a crumb on the floor

perchance, or not brewed her herbal tea to perfection again?

James turned off the taps. 'What?'

'Don't be with another.'

'Where the hell did that come from?'

'I have a sensitive nose, James.'

'You have a beautiful nose,' James said, 'as does our baby.'

'Don't change the subject.'

Should he tell her? James wondered. Should he just admit that he was trying to learn Arabic so that he could speak with her father, so he could somehow make things better for Leila and their child? That the scent she smelled was Nadir's rather unsubtle perfume.

No, because three weeks into learning Arabic and James was seriously wondering if his goal was achievable and he did not want her to know that he had failed.

'I would never cheat, Leila.' He was direct and honest; he just didn't give her all of the truth. 'A night with my parents only reinforces to me that I don't want a marriage like that.'

'Why did you rush into the shower?'

'I told you, I'm taking you on a date tonight.' He looked at her narrowed eyes. 'Could you go, please,' James said as she still stood there. 'Or you're welcome to get in.'

That got rid of her!

He came out to the sight of Leila in one of her new robes, a lilac one.

'You look stunning.'

'Thank you.'

Leila *felt* stunning. Her wardrobe was filled now with robes of soft lilacs and pinks and pale lemons—and they suited her far better than the silver and gold ones that she used to wear.

She felt like herself when she looked in the mirror.

James was looking immaculate too, and he had even shaved! He came up behind her and they looked at each other in the mirror.

'I'm planning something, Leila,' James said. 'And it has your best interests at heart, so when I'm vague, that's where I am. If you're going to jump to the possibility I'm cheating every time I don't tell you exactly where I've been, then expect boring presents and surprises at Christmas and birthdays.'

That mollified her a little. 'Where are you taking me?' Leila asked again.

To bed, James wanted to say but settled for, 'It's a surprise.'

'Am I overdressed?'

'Can a princess ever be overdressed?'

He looked at her body; her breasts were bigger and he ached to touch them. Her stomach at sixteen weeks was just becoming noticeable to others but they were both extraordinarily excited by the tiny swell.

Badly he wanted to touch her.

Badly she wanted him too.

'Come on,' James said. 'We can't be late.'

His driver dropped them at the Lincoln Center and still Leila did not have a clue. They walked past a lit-up fountain along with others to Avery Fisher Hall and still Leila did not know what was happening.

They had drinks and she smiled at his boredom with water when he asked the bartender for several slices of lime.

'Only for you would I do this.'

'Do what?'

'Give up drinking and come here...'

'James, what are we doing here standing drinking with all these people?'

He loved that all this was so alien to her,

and it was alien to him too, for he had never been a part of a couple.

'You're going to see the New York Philharmonic Orchestra,' James said. 'And I suspect you're going to love it.'

Oh, she did.

It could not have been better. Leila made music, but to have it made for her, to sit and listen, to hear instruments that she had never heard before, sent shivers right through her body.

Who knew music could be so sexy, James thought.

It turned out it was though. He could feel her enjoyment building beside him; now and then her hand would find his and her fingers would press into his in anticipation. Their calves met, their energy met; it was all in all the best and the most happily received surprise he had ever delivered.

'I loved it,' Leila said as they stepped outside all giddy and high from a night sitting side by side. 'Every minute of it.'

'Well, there will be many, many more.' He took out an envelope and Leila opened it.

'It's a season ticket,' James said. 'You can go to as many concerts as you like, but you can also go along to hear them rehearse.' As she opened her mouth he got there first. 'You can't join in,' James said.

'One day, maybe.'

'I don't know,' James said. 'I've never heard you play.'

He might just have to rectify that!

'Why are you so nice to me?' Leila asked as they got into bed that night.

'Because I am nice,' James said. 'And so are you.'

'I'm mean to the maids.'

'But you're getting better.'

They were getting better.

With each passing day they drew closer, and at night it was getting harder to hold back her heart. To not give in to the love she had for him. To not plead with him for seven decades, rather than seven years.

There were still tears in her sleep, and one Saturday morning when she was now eighteen weeks pregnant, finally he asked her about them.

'What do you dream of?' James asked as she lay there in his arms.

Leila had never told anyone, but here, with

his arms around her, it did not feel nosey or invasive.

'There are different dreams, though they all feel the same,' Leila said. 'I just dreamt that I was at a picnic. I could see my parents laughing. I am a little girl about seven or eight, and my brother and sister are there. We are all laughing and enjoying the conversation and then I realise they cannot hear what I am saying. That they are talking amongst themselves as if I am not there. I start to shout, and they just carry on talking and laughing. I knock over a glass and they do not turn their heads…I start screaming and crying…'

She was silent for a moment and James lay there thinking.

'That's when you come in,' Leila said, because it was when she sobbed that he stepped into her dream and held her.

She wasn't even sure if it was a dream or a memory. Leila thought back to times looking out of her window, watching her mother and Jasmine walking in the grounds side by side.

'Hey, Leila,' James said. 'Don't wait so long.'

'Sorry?'

'When you're dreaming and you knock the glass over, or you realise they can't hear you, just roll over in the bed to me.'

CHAPTER ELEVEN

'MANU!' JAMES HAD waited till Leila had left for work to make the call.

'I was wondering if you could come to meet with me here in New York. I want some help to deal with Leila's parents.'

'You certainly need it.'

'Which is why I want you to get on a plane as soon as possible.' James looked out to the view below as he spoke. He hated that Leila cried each night. Yes, he knew she had been unhappy enough to run away but that he might have caused an irretrievable breakdown between Leila and her family, so much so that they might want nothing to do with the baby, appalled him.

Dream interpretation wasn't his particular forte; in fact, he didn't even pay attention to his own. It was clear though, James had decided, that Leila was worried that her family was carrying on completely fine without her and that they might want nothing to do with their baby.

He wanted to do his best to put things right.

'I've been trying to learn Arabic so that I can hopefully apologise in person to her father.'

'It is more than the language you need to learn, James.'

'I get that.' He did not need a lecture from Manu and was just about to tell her so when the door opened and there was Leila.

'I'll call you back,' James said.

'No need,' Manu said. 'I'll arrange my flight. I can be there tomorrow for two days, but I am not guaranteeing I will work with you. For now I'll just agree to meet and discuss the situation. I'll text you with the times.'

'Did I disturb you?' Leila asked.

'Of course not,' James clipped. 'I was just moving some stocks...'

She knew that he was lying—Leila had heard a woman's voice on the other end of the phone.

She had sensitive ears too!

'How come you're not at work?' James asked.

'Their evening player has asked to swap and so I am working tonight instead,' Leila answered. 'I have to be back at six.'

'I don't want you…' James halted himself. Who was he to tell her that she couldn't work when she so clearly loved it? Who was he to rein her in when she was just starting to find herself?

And, James questioned, who was he to force her to marry him?

He just wanted her to want to now.

'Whatever you feel like doing,' James said.

'Anyway, clearly we need to have some time alone,' Leila said. 'To make our private phone calls and things.'

James heard the little dig and he gave a wry smile as Leila huffed off to the bathroom.

She was the most adorable creature of habit—as soon as she came home, she would remove her make-up and he followed her in, watching as she took out a make-up–remover wipe. Leila started taking off her mascara but he could see the angry strokes of her hands.

She was jealous, James thought, but it made him smile for she had no reason to be.

'Leila.' He came behind her and tried to catch her eye in the mirror but she was deliberately ignoring him.

'Leila…' James slid a hand around her waist but she shrugged him off and so he sat on the marble vanity beside where she stood angrily taking off her make-up.

'Just because I'm on the phone to a woman it doesn't mean that I'm seeing someone else. You are the most insecure person I have ever met.'

'I'm not insecure, James,' Leila corrected. 'I'm very secure with myself.'

'You could try trusting me.'

Leila breathed out. Yes, she could try trusting; it just felt like a scary place to be. She wanted to trust him; she wanted to believe that he was here for more than their baby, that somehow a marriage between them could work.

She wanted to tell him that she loved him.

He handed her another make-up wipe and she took it.

'I'm your personal make-up remover assistant,' James said, and watched her lips do their best not to smile.

She liked him in the bathroom with her, how he even made taking off her make-up stupid fun.

He picked up her moisturiser and squeezed some onto his fingers.

Sexy fun, Leila amended, remembering those fingers removing her lipstick that night, and so she rather pointedly took the bottle from him and put on her own moisturiser.

Not fazed, happy to sit, James's eyes alit on the pills in her bag.

'Fat lot of good they did,' James said, but not unkindly, and that was enough to bring that reluctant smile to her lips.

Idly he picked them up as Leila finished off her face.

'Leila…' James asked. 'Where did you get these pills?'

Leila hesitated, for even in death she tried to protect Jasmine's reputation. 'From a doctor.'

'Okay,' James said, 'let's rephrase that. *When* did you get these pills?'

'I can't remember.'

'They expired years ago.' Good God, James

thought as he read the date on them again—they had actually expired more than a decade ago!

'Expired?'

He handed her the packet and pointed to the date and he saw her frown. 'Medicines expire,' James said, 'in the same way that food does. Don't you look at the top of your yoghurt…' And he stopped then because what would Leila know about expiry dates and such like. 'They go off. These pills wouldn't work now.'

She felt stupid, embarrassed; she felt naive and very sure that he would be cross with her.

'I didn't know,' Leila whimpered in panic. She was instantly back to the time in her bathroom with her chopped hair on the floor beside her and she was ashamed. 'I was wrong…'

'It's okay,' James said. He got that she simply didn't know. What he didn't get was that her eyes were filling with tears and that Leila, who only cried at night, who rarely revealed herself to him, was starting to break down. 'Leila, it's fine,' James said. 'I'm not cross. I get that it was a mistake…' He gave her a smile and regrettably made just a little dig.

'Though it's a mistake that only you could make.'

He was appalled as she crumpled.

'They were Jasmine's,' Leila sobbed. 'They belonged to Jasmine. I had hidden them for her.'

'Your sister who died?' James checked, and Leila nodded. She never really spoke about them; she just tried to halt things when he asked questions about her family, but he asked a direct one now. 'How long ago did that happen?'

'Sixteen years ago.'

He had assumed, just from the little she had told him, that whatever had happened had been a couple of years ago. That her mother had not been able to look at her since then appalled James.

Sixteen years was a helluva long time to be ignored.

She started crying then, really crying, and James took her to the lounge and, through tears, she told him some of her truth.

'Jasmine had a trunk that I hid in my dressing room. The night I left Surhaadi, I had an argument with my mother. I was going to show her that Jasmine had been up to no good when she died, but then I decided to use those things on me instead. Everything that night was Jasmine's—the clothes, the shoes, the make-up. I was trying to be her…' She waited for the repercussions, for the crack of the whip. For him to tell her what a fool she was, for that was all she was used to, but when he spoke it was not in anger.

'That's pretty messed up, Leila,' James said. And then she looked up and she could not believe that he gently smiled as he carried on speaking. 'So I was making out with the ghost of Jasmine?'

How could he touch on such a painful subject and not hurt her further?

'No,' Leila said. 'I stopped trying to be her when I met you.'

Why wasn't he telling her she was stupid? Instead his hand was at her cheek, wiping away a tear, and he revealed a fear of his own.

'I go over and over that night,' James said. 'I'm terrified that if I hadn't been there what might have happened to you, because despite what everyone thinks, I *did* take care of you that night.'

'You did,' Leila said. 'And no, it could only have been you. As I walked into that bar I had realised just how mad it was.' She took a big breath and said the bravest words of her life. 'And then I saw you. It could only have been you because had you not turned around when you did, then I would have run back to my suite. I would have taken off those clothes. I would have gone back to my parents and tried to somehow make it work, except I walked towards you.'

'Good.' James smiled. 'I can breathe better now.'

'I got us into this mess.'

'Where's the mess?' James asked, and she looked deeply into his eyes and there was no mess to be seen. 'The best thing that ever happened to me was the night you walked into that room.' James admitted it not just to Leila but to himself. 'We made a baby and while it's taken some getting used to I don't see that as a mess. You're going to be an amazing mother. I'm going to do all I can to be the best father that I can be. I've never taken something more seriously in my life. I promise you, I will sort things out with your parents.'

'You can't,' Leila said. 'Please don't make me a promise that you cannot keep. I want to ring my mother but I am too scared. I don't want to know that she's disowned me and that she might want nothing to do with my child.' Leila let out a breath. 'Maybe if I have a girl and call her Jasmine...'

'Okay, let's not make any decisions about that yet,' James said hastily, because the more he heard about Jasmine the less he liked her. 'I'll try to at least not make things any worse with your parents, but I do promise you that I won't cheat. Can you believe that much?'

Almost.

She wanted to believe that much, that this beautiful man actually wanted her, that love was coming into her life.

'I'll try.'

'Bloody hell,' James said. 'Best speech of my life, lukewarm reception.' He gave her his smile. 'I'll take it.'

Leila had her sleep and James played the stock market, but every now and then he looked over to where she was sleeping, and at five, he called her name.

'You've got work.'

'I know.'

'Now, I know that I'm going to sound really chauvinist,' James said, 'but I don't want you working nights, not because I don't want you working nights but because...'

'I don't want to go in either.' Leila smiled because she wanted tonight to be with him.

'Can you call in sick?'

'No.'

'You can.'

'I won't do that to them,' Leila said, and took a breath, 'though I was thinking of telling them that I won't be coming back,' Leila admitted. 'Maybe on occasions but I like that season ticket that you got me for the orchestra and I love watching them rehearse.'

It was the biggest compliment she could give him, that this very independent princess might trust him enough to take care of her.

'Tell them that this is your last night,' James said.

Which meant, if he wanted to hear her play, then he'd be going along tonight too.

James took a turn on the bed as Leila showered. She came out of the bathroom and dried herself in front of him and she did not turn her back and James did not move. Leila went over to the dressing table and took out her underwear that she had chosen and bought for herself and put them on and then did her make-up.

And he still did not move.

Leila walked over to the wardrobe and selected her favourite new robe, in the palest mint green. She slithered it on and then she met his eyes.

'Are you going to offer to help with the buttons?'

'Nope.'

Leila put her arms behind her back and looked at him watching her body as she struggled with the small buttons.

'Will you help me with my buttons?'

There was no *please* but he jerked his head and she went over and turned around and stood holding her hair up as he sat on the edge of the bed.

'Please?' James said, watching the spread of colour on the back of her neck.

'Please,' Leila said.

For every button her spine got a kiss, for every kiss her thighs loosened till he easily pulled her to his lap to do the last buttons to her neck. When they were done he did not turn her to face him; he just pulled her further back into his lap and his mouth met the heat of her neck.

She wanted to turn but his hands held her hips, and his mouth was at the back of her ear so she could both feel and hear his ragged breathing as she pressed back into him.

'I'll call in sick...' Leila offered, and not just for him!

'It would be wrong to let them down at the last minute,' James said as he released her from his knee.

She stood, but did not meet his eyes, and as she put on her veil and left she did not ask what he would be doing tonight while she was working.

They both knew where this night would lead.

Leila told the manager and Habib that this would be her last night playing at the restaurant and the manager let out a sigh. He had been expecting it, not just because he had worked out that she was the fiancée of James Chatsfield, but because of the way Leila played he had known that they would not have her for long. More and more the clients were asking for her. More and more the restaurant grew quiet as she played.

'You'll come and see us though?' he checked.

'Of course,' Leila said. 'I love dining here.'

The restaurant was very busy and at first Leila quietly played. She did not look up, yet she knew the very moment that James walked in.

She heard the murmur of the guests as a very well-known man entered, but more than that her heart knew and for a moment her fingers, which had never missed a note, faltered.

James heard the silence and then breathed out as her gentle playing resumed.

He was guided to a small low table that had a *shisha* pipe and many plates. James took a seat on the cushions and he told the waitress that no, he wasn't expecting anyone to join him.

He did not dine alone though, for her music spoke to him the whole night.

It did.

And it did not just speak to him, because as her music intensified, the guests started to work out that the mysterious beauty must surely be James Chatsfield's fiancée, for why else would he be watching her so intently and with pride in his eyes as Leila told their story with her fingers.

James heard of the fear and confusion that had spun her into the sky that night and had brought her to New York.

He recognised the moment they met for there were two harmonies now coming from her fingers. Masculine and feminine, playing alongside, complementing the other, strengthening the other, enhancing the other.

Their first kiss she captured and so, too, their first dance.

The restaurant was entranced as she gave them her and James's story.

Did they know, James wondered, that Leila was telling them now of the night they had first made love?

Did they get the pain that was being revealed to him now, as he left her alone in a hotel room?

Could they understand her fingers spoke of confusion and fear that ran alongside the joy of knowing a baby was growing inside of her?

Her music spoke of them again, of those tentative first days together, that had since spread into weeks. It told of anger that faded and rows that healed rather than hurt. It told of faltering steps towards intimate moments, but it did not say the one thing that now needed to be said.

Rather abruptly the music concluded and Leila looked up and met his eyes.

The restaurant broke into spontaneous applause. Leila had never been applauded for her music and it was somewhat overwhelming, but the best part of it was when they stepped outside and James told her he had been wrong.

'You could raise ten babies on your music, Leila. You were amazing.'

'Thank you.'

'It was about us, wasn't it?'

'No.' Leila smiled. 'You must have had too much *shisha*.' She pointed to a café that was closed. 'That is where I get my coffee after my shift and then I take it over to the park and I watch the people and I dream.'

'What do you dream?'

'That I belong.'

'We could go over there now.'

'It's nighttime,' Leila said.

'But you're not alone,' James said. 'And you do belong.'

She'd always been alone, Leila thought, yet she didn't feel that she was now.

They walked through the dark and she led him to a bench where she usually sat, but tonight they decided that they would lie on the grass and they looked up to the stars.

'There are so few,' Leila said. 'Where I live there are millions…'

'There are millions here also,' James said. 'There are just too many lights in the city to be able to see them.'

'You're a very nice teacher,' Leila said, because he never made her feel stupid. 'You are very patient in the way you explain things to me.'

He turned and looked at her. 'Do you miss home?'

Leila did not look back at him; instead she stared up at the sky and wondered how he would react if she told him that this was home now, that he was her home. That the affection and the care he had shown to her these past weeks, even during the most trying of times, was more than she had known in her life.

She didn't answer him; it was James who broke the long silence

'*I* miss home,' James said, and he watched as she turned to him. 'I've got an apartment about a ten-minute walk from here. I honestly thought we'd do better in the hotel—you know, dinner in the restaurant...'

'We don't go down for dinner much though.'

'No,' James said. 'And I'm starting to really enjoy having breakfast in bed.' Their gazes held. 'With you.'

'I am too,' Leila admitted.

He leant up on his elbow and his hand was on her cheek. 'Come and live with me, Leila, in my home.'

'You *want* to live with me?'

'I could think of nothing nicer,' James said, and his mouth came down on hers.

Soft and slow, he kissed her, and it was Leila whose tongue slipped in first.

She was deeply in love with him, Leila knew. She wanted the endearments, wanted more of the kiss he gave. His hand was resting on the ground by her head, hers was at the back of his head. She knew every part of where their minds and bodies were when he pulled his lips away with just enough breath to say the words she had longed to hear—'I'm in love with you.'

And she was in love with him too. In this space that was theirs, that had been found by them.

'I loved you from that first night,' Leila admitted.

'I know that now,' James said, and so he knew just how badly he had hurt her. 'There were no clothes, no make-up, no phone number. I thought you were a journalist, or someone that Isabelle had set me up with to trick me…'

His hand was stroking her breast, and when he told her what had happened, she simply better understood that morning now. She wasn't scared to tell him that he was right, that Zayn's new girlfriend at the time had been the spy who had exposed their names to the media, just not now, not yet.

It wasn't needed.

They were in love and he was taking her home.

CHAPTER TWELVE

HE WALKED HER past the doorman and through the elegant foyer and Leila looked up at the huge chandelier and then to a row of brass-gated elevators. There was a gleaming walnut table in the centre, as big as any at the palace, and the flowers that sat atop it rivalled the palace flowers too.

There were beautiful shops and bars and restaurants and there was a very well-dressed elderly-couple walking in front of them, clearly back from a night out and arguing loudly.

It was busy, it was exciting—even this late at night.

Yes, Leila *loved* Manhattan.

'Meet the neighbours,' James said with a nudge.

'Esther and Matthew, this is Leila...' James

introduced her as they stepped in the elevator and there was that pride in his voice again.

The couple said hello and then carried on rowing till they got out on the seventh floor, though they paused to wish James and Leila goodnight.

She hadn't even seen his home but she loved it already.

To the top they went and he felt that it was important to make one small point. 'You're the first woman I've brought here.'

'And the last,' Leila said, but assuredly now, then she smiled.

She didn't know where she was; she just knew she was in heaven. A tour could wait—they had been turning the other on long before the park—and he took her straight to his bedroom.

She was shaking when he turned her around and his voice was deliciously impatient as he struggled with those buttons. 'Can we get zips fitted to your gowns?'

'Yes.'

She was so perfect, the dress was so perfect, that he did not tear it. He was undressing her as best he could as he undid the buttons right to the end and she slipped her robe off.

'I'm never wearing socks again,' James said as he took them off and she dealt with her bra.

And then he turned her around, both now naked right to their hearts. They kissed, and James's hands took in the swell of her stomach, and the heavier weight of her breasts were finally his to explore. First his fingers grew familiar with her body and then his mouth and tongue joined the caress too. His bed was like lying on a pillow, Leila thought as he swirled one thick nipple with his tongue and slid his fingers into her.

'James…' She wanted to clamp her thighs together, as deep within her he found another sensitive spot. Delighted with her response, James parted her thighs further. Leila lay trembling with the torture of it as he explored her deeply—his fingers massaging her on the inside as his mouth suckled her clitoris until she sobbed with the delicious hurt, her hands tightening around his wrist, almost dragging him from her as he brought her to a deep orgasm.

She had been scared to make love for this reason, because he simply owned her when they did, but she knew that she owned his heart too, because when she went to kiss him he rolled her onto him.

'Get on top—I want to see you.'

And it meant, Leila found out, that she got to see him too.

It was Leila's second time dancing and this time it was with him inside. His hands held her hips loosely enough that she could move as she wished, and there was nothing crude about this belly dance.

Slowly she worked out what worked for her and he was as patient as he always had been.

She loved the freedom he gave her, the feel of his hands on her breasts as he started to match her moves and lift into Leila.

Leila liked the feel of his eyes on her; she liked how sexy he made her feel and that she could touch her own breasts as he played with the magic spot he had discovered in her.

She felt hotter than she did when working at the restaurant, more breathless than she did when her temper rose.

She loved the hard work of him, the grittiness of being allowed to be herself as she moved over and over his thick length.

He started tweaking at her nipples and in a tease Leila leant forward, her hands either side of his head, her full breast over his mouth, and she found out then that his patience wasn't infinite because James's hands were back on her hips and starting to pull her down faster.

He could feel her building, just as he had on the dance floor. For now, he knew her sexually better than Leila knew herself, but not for long, James knew.

Even as she tried to tell him *not yet*, James made her a liar because she was lifting her head and arching her back, pressing her hands to his chest as she came to his body's command.

Her scream was the first she had knowingly given; it felt like she was on the top of a mountain, dragging in the thin air and spinning as James took her to a place that only he ever could.

She had been searching for freedom, Leila realised. But not the decadent kind. Instead she had been seeking the freedom that the love of another gave and she had found it now in James.

CHAPTER THIRTEEN

A NIGHT WITHOUT TEARS.

Her first one.

James watched the smile spread on Leila's face as she woke and looked out of the huge window to the spectacular view of Central Park. She could see the lake where she often walked, the beautiful trees and the lush grass where they had lain last night.

'Wait till you see it in fall,' James said. 'It never gets old.'

'What is it like in winter?'

'Spectacular,' James said. 'Especially when it snows overnight and you weren't expecting it.'

She thought of tasting snow on her tongue in the taxi rank and knew that somehow she had been on her way to here.

'Do you have dinner parties with your family here?' Leila asked.

'No,' James said. 'They came over once when I first bought it and my father said that had I spoken to him, he could have got a better price in another building and a better view too.'

'There is no better view,' Leila said.

'I said the same to him.'

'Do you wish you were closer to them?' Leila asked, and James thought for a little while before he answered her.

'I used to when I was growing up but I finally worked out it wasn't worth wasting my time. I didn't run away quite as dramatically as you. In fact, I haven't even left town, but really, apart from the odd get-together I'm done with them. We're runaways,' James said.

'I like being on the run. We'll never move?'

'Never, though we'll have to baby-proof it,' James said, and then rolled his eyes, because he never, ever thought he'd be saying that about his home. 'Do you want a tour?'

Together they explored his home. There were views of the park from every window, there were bedrooms and bathrooms and just all things James—such as a bedroom with the cupboard filled with skis and things.

'This is your room,' James said, and showed her the kitchen.

'Ha, ha,' Leila said, because she got his sarcasm now. 'You will go very, very hungry if you wait for me to cook, and you don't want to hear about when I tried to do dishes.' She did make concessions though. 'Show me how this works.'

James pressed a button on the kettle. 'But there has to be water in it.'

They were so happy that even boiling a kettle was a celebration, but when he showed her another room, Leila thought she might cry. It was empty apart from a shelf that had a silver teddy on, the one he had bought when he had got her engagement ring.

It was another happiest day of her life; every day with him turned into that.

All her clothes and belongings were brought over from The Chatsfield, and James had staff put them away, right down to the last pair of shoes.

She was in, she was home, and the best part for James was, that night there were, again, no tears.

They overslept, of course.

James's phone bleeped a text and he found

out from a rather irate Manu that he was half an hour late for their meeting.

'I have to go,' James said.

'Where?'

'I've got meetings at The Chatsfield over the next couple of days,' James lightly explained. 'I'll call Muriel and tell her to come in tomorrow so you can get your bearings today.'

'Who's Muriel?'

'She takes care of the place,' James said. 'She just comes in once a week while I'm away, but now I'm back she'll come in daily, just for an hour or two. Well, not at the weekends.'

'No cook?'

'I told you, you can ring the restaurants downstairs.'

'Just one person for a couple of hours a day?'

'Is that a problem?'

'No.' Leila smiled. 'It's wonderful.'

As he showered he thought about them and as he put on his suit he told her some of what he'd been thinking. After sixteen years of being ignored, James doubted his stilted Arabic could solve that in any conversation with her parents, but her brother kept trying to contact her and maybe *there*, there was something that he could do. 'What about your brother?' James asked when he came out. 'Why don't you make contact with him? He does seem to be trying to speak with you.'

'I'm not talking to Zayn for what he did to you.'

'Well, I didn't appreciate it at the time but I get why he did what he did now. What if I spoke to him?' James said, while not particularly relishing the thought, and he watched her guilty swallow.

'I have something to tell you.'

Finally, James thought. 'Please do,' he said.

'It is something that might make you cross.'

'Do tell!'

'It was Sophie who revealed our names to the press.'

'Zayn's wife?'

'She had her reasons to do so, Zayn said. Something to do with Jasmine, but I was so cross that I told them I didn't want to hear their excuses.' He was putting on his tie and seemed as bothered with what she'd said as if she'd told him it had just started raining outside. 'I'm worried what it will do to us,' Leila admitted.

'To us?' James grinned. 'Why would it affect us? Does the fact my father is, and I quote, "vile", make you think less of me?'

'Of course not.'

'So, don't worry about it. God, if you think we're going to row every time one of our family members stuffs up, then marrying me might not be such a good idea.'

She smiled at his reaction. 'You're like no one I've ever met.'

'Snap,' James said.

'Snap,' replied Leila.

'I was right though,' James said as he finished his tie. 'Isabelle did have someone on me. I knew it!' he said. 'I knew I was being followed.'

She laughed when he lifted the trousers of his immaculate suit a few inches. 'Look, no socks.'

He gave her a lovely kiss before leaving and Leila lay back happily in his bed, looking out at the view of Central Park.

Surely she belonged now.

* * *

James and Manu had never really got on but he did accept that she knew her stuff.

They headed to the near-empty restaurant and to a table in the far corner, where they ordered breakfast, but five minutes into his meeting with her James started to question getting Manu involved.

'Leila's happy…'

'Really?'

'She is,' James said *'We're* happy. It's just her parents that are proving a problem and her brother.'

'I wonder why that might be!'

'She hasn't got on with her parents since her sister died. I'm thinking of approaching her brother…' James attempted to explain, but again Manu shook her head.

'Let's get back to Leila…'

James actually had Leila Deficit Disorder because one hour out of bed and he needed contact, but he was aware of his own arrogance and also needed to be sure he was right.

Are you happy? James texted.

So, so happy! Leila replied, and James

smiled and simply forgot that Manu was there.

Go and look at the bottom of the wardrobe.

Leila texted him back. A present?

Just go and look.

There was nothing there though. She looked up on the shelves and there were just cases and shoes and so she checked the bottom of the wardrobe again and there was nothing there either, save a shirt that had fallen from the hanger.

No, Leila realised, it hadn't fallen from the hanger. It was wrinkled and hadn't been laundered.

Her heart skipped in hope and she knew they had found love that night for he had kept it. She buried her face in it and smelled not just the musk of herself but the citrus note to the cologne that he wore and the masculine scent that was James.

I'm wearing it now!

Send me a picture! James replied as Manu droned on.

It was the tamest picture of a woman in bed that James had ever received but it was by far his favourite—Leila sitting up in bed wearing the shirt and smiling brightly for him and lightly he teased her. Undo the top button at least!

'You are so insolent, James,' Manu said, and James looked up and for a moment he wondered if she had been standing over his shoulder and reading his phone, but Manu didn't need to read what was written. James realised that he had been very rudely ignoring her.

'Look, I apologise, I honestly…'

He didn't know how to explain that he was *in* love, in *serious* love, and just so open to Leila-distraction at the moment. How did he tell Manu, who was looking at him with such distaste, that he had never felt anything like it before?

'You're just a rich boy who is far too used to getting whatever it is that he wants,' Manu sneered.

'Not necessarily.' James commenced a smart reply, but then he remembered why he was here and swallowed his retort down. 'I just want Leila to be happy.'

'You just said that she was.'

Well, apart from her wish for her parents to at least not take things out on their child and that she was estranged from her brother. Apart from the tears she sobbed each night, but since she'd been in his home they had stopped.

'You cause offence at every turn,' Manu said.

There was that bloody word again.

When he was with Leila, when it was just the two of them, it was all so uncomplicated. Yet, James conceded, Leila hadn't responded to his flirt. She hadn't sent another text. Perhaps he *had* offended and so James pocketed his phone.

Manu now had his full attention and what she had to say was sobering indeed.

Oh, he so did not cause offence.

Leila had actually laughed at James's text. No, she would not be unbuttoning to her phone, but he made her so happy that she felt brave.

Brave enough to handle anything.

Leila picked up her phone and stared, but not at James's texts. She went to the address book and to where James had keyed her parents' number into the phone.

She looked at the time in Surhaadi, as James had added a clock with the time there.

It was after dinnertime now.

She knew that the phone rang in the lounge where they had had that terrible row and knew that they would be sitting there now.

Leila held her breath as a maid answered it.

'I wish to speak with my mother,' Leila said, and when she heard the shocked gasp, Leila remembered her new manners with maids. 'Please.'

It took ages for her mother to come to the phone—no doubt she would be shooing out all the servants—and Leila waited.

And she waited.

Leila was starting to wish she had done this when James was here because he had helped her to forget a little how her mother's spite made her feel.

She was starting to remember it now.

It was the same maid who came back to the phone.

'She says that whoever you are you are

a cruel trickster for her only daughter died many years ago.'

Leila cleared her throat before speaking. 'Tell my mother that if she will speak with me this once, then, if it is her wish, she will never have to speak with me again.'

Leila closed her eyes and waited and finally her mother came to the phone.

'*Sharmota.*' Her mother called her a whore, which Leila had expected given all that had happened.

'Mother, please,' Leila calmly attempted. 'I know it seems terrible but James is a wonderful man and we are getting married. You know that we are having a baby, please think about it—this will be your first grandchild...' Leila played the best card she had. 'If it is a girl we shall call her...'

'Your dirty street bastard is no relation to me.'

And something rose in Leila as her mother spoke like that about the tiny baby that grew inside her.

'I am not ringing because I need your approval, Mother. I am just calling to let you know that I am safe and that I am loved.'

'Loved?' Farrah's voice was incredulous.

'Yes, loved,' Leila said. 'James loves me.'

'He told you that?'

'He did.'

Oh, she tried, how she tried to stand up to her, but even the bed seemed to shake beneath her and Leila clung to the sheet with one hand and tried to resist being dragged back to the mad vortex that she had fought so hard to escape from.

'Did he tell you he loved you just before you parted your legs or during?' her mother asked and Leila screwed her eyes closed. 'Because he does not love you, Leila. Tell me, please, why would he?'

'He just does,' Leila said.

'But why?'

Leila's conviction wavered and she could not answer at first, so she sought James's words. 'I'll be an amazing mother...'

'As I said, you are not my daughter. There are no portraits on the walls of you anymore.' She had been removed, Leila realised, and she thought of herself standing and looking at the portraits and now any one with her in it was gone. She had simply been deleted from their lives. 'Don't worry for us,' her mother continued, 'the palace is happier now without you. Your father has started taking evening walks again, which he has not done since Jasmine's death. I have started a new tapestry. Even the maids smile more as they go about their day. We are better without you.'

James arrived home to find Leila in bed and he was just about to say that that she was just where he liked to find her when he saw her face, which was whiter than the shirt she wore.

'Leila?'

She shook her head—she could not tell him, she could not find her voice. But he could taste the grief in the room.

'The baby?' James asked.

Leila shook her head again and tried to remember how her voice worked. 'I spoke with my mother...' and that was all she could say.

'When?'

Leila didn't answer but James had already worked it out. At first he had thought he might have caused offence when she didn't respond to his flirt. And after eight hours being lectured by Manu as to just how offensive he could be at times, James had been certain that was why she hadn't responded to his text. Now though he knew the truth.

She had been like this for hours, James realised, just lying on the bed with her pain.

'Go,' Leila said.

'I can't.'

'Please.'

He made it to the kitchen and found some green tea bags, which were the only remotely herbal thing James had, and added some honey, no doubt from the wrong bees, and brought it in to her.

'It's nice,' Leila said, and sipped the hot tea.

'I didn't have orange blossom honey though,' James said. 'We'll have to do a Leila shop tomorrow.'

It was the saddest thing he had ever seen—watching her trying and failing to smile for him.

He got undressed and got into bed; no sex was going to fix this and so he held her instead.

Don't disown me, she wanted to say.

Please don't hurt me.

Please don't come home stinking of perfume.

Even pretend to love me, just never let me know that you don't.

Her mother's words had more than stung, they had crushed, and she didn't know what to believe anymore.

His hand was on her stomach, the reason he was here perhaps.

'She called the baby a dirty street bastard,' Leila finally spoke.

'Excuse me!' James said, perhaps a little too loudly for her fragile state, but as the baby kicked and she realised he was talking on behalf of the baby, now Leila managed a pale smile. 'I think someone's rather offended,' James said as the baby kicked again, and he rubbed her stomach. 'Tell your mother,' he said to their child, 'that we can fix that and I'll marry her any day that she wants.'

'You can't fix this, James.'

No, but he could make contact with Zayn, James thought, especially when later she cried in the night, for so wretched were her tears.

He was up and dressed and certainly he would not be late for Manu this morning.

'I've got meetings till six,' James said,

knowing that Manu flew back tonight. 'Will you be okay?'

'We have the ultrasound at two.'

'Of course we do.' James eyes briefly shuttered. 'I'll meet you there at ten to two.'

He'd forgotten, Leila decided.

He paused; a part of him wanted to tell her his plans, but the other part of him that was terrified of promising something he could not achieve was confirmed when he met a stony-faced Manu in the foyer of The Chatsfield.

'What the hell?' Manu demanded.

She handed him a newspaper and James looked. Their kiss in Central Park had been captured—even worse, his hand was on her breast.

'I didn't think anyone was around…'

'We're not discussing this here,' Manu said. 'I've booked a business suite on the seventeenth floor.'

Manu swiped the door and they stepped into the suite and then set straight to work. Manu took the newspaper from him and James didn't really need to be told how bad it looked.

'I didn't know there was anyone nearby and certainly not someone with a camera.'

'Your hand is on her breast,' Manu said. 'While I get that you want to fool the public here that your relationship is real, talk about a slap in the face for her parents and for her brother…'

James blew out. He wasn't trying to fool anyone now; he and Leila had moved far past all that.

'You get their virgin daughter pregnant,' Manu said, and it felt like judgment day. 'You leave her alone to deal with it and have been seen with other women since then…' She just spelled it out and James could see the disgust in Manu's eyes. 'Yes, you propose and then you make out with her in the park.'

'It was a kiss that went too far.'

'Any kiss in public is a kiss that has gone too far. It is not just this kiss. You walk in the street holding her hand—that must only happen behind the closed doors of your home. Can't you see that everything you do just further insults not only her family, it insults Leila. You're not even married…'

'About that, I don't know if I should try and speak with her brother before or after we marry…' James started, and then he hesitated. Forcing Leila into marriage had seemed so straightforward at the time; it had been about protecting his baby, yet even that made less sense now.

'I'm going to discuss things with Leila,' James said. 'I'm going to sort out what it is that she wants. But if we do marry...'

'Then you would need to meet face to face with her father, though I doubt that he would receive you.'

'What about her brother?'

'You would need a mediator, someone to approach him on your behalf.'

'Someone like you?' James said, but his smile was met with cold eyes.

'Do you know why I'm so expensive, James? It is because I have a very good reputation in the business world. I don't know if I want my name attached to you if you offend the king again in a year or so.'

'I'm not going to cause any offence,' James said.

'Oh, so this marriage is going to last?' Manu checked. 'You're going to be faithful...'

'Why is everyone so sure that I'm going to cheat?'

'You're a Chatsfield,' Manu said. 'Oh, and you're *James* Chatsfield.'

As his rather depraved past caught up with him, James simply sat there. He had always been able to charm his way out of anything, buy his way out of anything…just not so easily in this, the one thing that mattered the most to him.

'It's going to take a lot of work, James,' Manu warned. 'A serious lot of work. I will think about acting as a medium for you with Leila's brother but I want to see you put in some effort before I do. If you want to help Leila to rebuild her relationship with her family, then you need to sit up and listen.'

James did.

He listened and he tried to take it all in.

He did it for Leila, not that she knew it.

Instead, at five minutes past two, she stood on the street outside the OB's and tried to tell herself not to overreact because he was late.

'I had an appointment,' James said as he got out of his car. 'It dragged on.'

He didn't kiss her; he didn't take her hand as they walked into the waiting room. He just sat there as they waited for her name to be called.

He glanced to Leila and to where her gaze fell—to the coffee table with today's newspaper on it and there they were, kissing with his hand on her breast.

'Leila...' James said. 'I apologise for that. I know that things went too far and if I in any way...'

'Apologise?' Leila demanded. 'How could you ever say sorry for that night? Anyway, it is not so bad. Muriel tells me that she has seen far worse from people in your very building.'

'Ah, so you've met Muriel.'

Leila certainly had. Muriel had blue hair and spoke nonstop. She had come in to where Leila lay curled up in bed and had told Leila if she wanted the bed made up, then she'd better get out of it!

Leila had sat in a chair as the maid cleaned around her. Then Muriel had proceeded to tell Leila about some of the goings-on in the very building where she was living. 'At least it was your breasts he was playing with,' Muriel had said as Leila got back in the fresh bed. 'Don't get me started on my ex!'

Now, sitting in the waiting room, Leila got that Muriel must have assumed that Leila had seen the newspapers.

'She's wonderful,' Leila said. 'But does she ever stop talking?'

'Never.' James smiled.

'Princess Al-Ahmar.'

James took in a tense breath, not just at the interruption, but at the use of her title. He had mocked Zayn that night in the alley and told him that here in New York he was royalty.

James better understood the tightening of Zayn's hand around his throat now.

'Do you want me to come in with you?' he offered, trying to remember some of what Manu had told him.

'Isn't that why you're here?' Leila said, and stalked off.

Everything had changed and Leila simply didn't know why. For, instead of coming over and sitting beside her, James stood back.

The chase was over, Leila decided as she lay there staring at the ceiling. She had given up her job, had moved in with him and she had admitted her love.

He knew that he had her heart now.

As the obstetrician lifted Leila's gown James saw the swell of her stomach and a small flash of pubic hair as she tucked in a towel and James shifted his gaze and looked to the wall.

But then he heard it—the sound of their baby's heartbeat—and he looked to the screen. He'd expected to see little but there it was, their baby, with one arm lifting and moving its tiny hand to its face. Hands, feet and there was that perfect nose. James wanted to go over; he wanted to sit at Leila's head and kiss her. He wanted to touch her stomach and the baby within, but instead he stood there.

'Did you want to know what you are having,' Catherine asked.

'Whatever Leila wants,' James said.

'I'd like to know,' Leila said, and she looked from the screen to James, and watched his eyes close as they were told they were expecting a girl.

A girl.

He'd accepted responsibility the second he had found out, but faced with the reality that he was going to be a father to a daughter had James reeling as he recalled the many mistakes he had made.

His head was spinning.

Everything he had done, he had seemingly done wrong. From the gaudy over-the-top engagement to the passionate kiss the other night.

No.

Leila was right—why the hell would he apologise for the best night of their lives?

He looked at the dark shadows under Leila's eyes as she lay on the examination table—it was her mother who had put them there, not he.

James was sure of that, just not quite sure enough.

He could almost feel himself being smacked upside the head for thinking he might have got something right as Leila walked out to the street with him.

'Are you disappointed that it is a girl?' Leila asked as they stepped outside.

'Disappointed?' James said. 'No, of course I'm not. I'm thrilled that we're having a girl.'

'Because if you wanted a boy…'

'Leila.' He picked up her hand and he watched her fingers close around his and he listened to his heart. He was sick of all the schools of thought and words of wisdom as to the unsuitability of them.

He was going to go back now and tell Manu thanks very much but he'd got this now.

'I have to go, Leila,' James said. 'Go home and have your rest. I won't be gone long and when I'm back we'll have a proper talk.'

'About?'

'Us,' James said. He gave her his smile but he did not take her into his arms. He would discuss what was appropriate with Leila later, but he squeezed her hand. 'Leila, I'm thrilled that it's a girl. I'm stunned. I never thought we'd get to see her as clearly as we did.'

James saw her into the car and Leila sat there. She turned her head and watched him walk briskly off.

As his driver headed towards his home, Leila's head too was spinning. Her mother had got into her head again and simply would not leave. Those seeds of doubt that James had had when he had dined at his parents that night were in Leila's head now. They hadn't just been given a decent soaking though—noxious weeds were flourishing and Leila would not wait till the master returned to find out what it was that he cared to discuss with her.

Instead it was time to be brave.

She did what she hadn't had the courage to on the first night she had arrived in New York.

When the car pulled up at James's home, instead of getting out she remained seated and spoke to the driver.

'Take me to The Chatsfield.'

CHAPTER FOURTEEN

MANU WAS THERE when James returned. She was waiting for him in reception, and speaking with some of the staff that she knew.

'I'm just waiting on a call from the Dubai hotel,' Manu said, and James nodded.

Spencer was passing through and came over and asked James if he'd made any plans for the wedding.

'I'll let you know,' James said, while privately deciding he'd perhaps tell his family well after the event.

Once Manu was ready they took the elevator in silence up to the suite. James had no issue with letting her go but, given how he might want to keep her onside, he was working out how best to tell her that her services were, for now, not required.

He might need her to speak with Zayn after all.

'I'm going to go home now and talk with Leila,' James said.

'I thought you wanted to work on this,' Manu said. 'I have to go back to Dubai tonight.'

'I know that,' James said, 'and while I do appreciate all your help, I need to discuss things with Leila.'

'You need my help, James. How is your Arabic going?'

'Absolutely terrible.' James told her a few of the phrases that he had learned and Manu laughed at his attempts to speak from the back of his throat, just as James expected her to, just as his father would too.

'Well, I'm glad it amuses you so much,' James said.

'You've got a very long way to go.' Manu could not stop laughing but James did not feel smacked upside the head this time. He was sick of the lot of them. 'Oh, James, thank you for the laugh. I needed it.'

Leila wouldn't laugh.

He knew that now.

What he didn't know though was that at this very moment he was breaking the heart of the woman he loved.

* * *

Leila had walked into the reception unseen by James and Manu. She had watched them walk over to the elevators and had hoped upon hope that this was not what it looked like.

Leila tried to trust him, tried to tell herself that he wouldn't take another woman to a bed that they had shared.

She watched the light on the elevator stop at the seventeenth floor instead of the top one and she pressed it and watched in dismay as the elevator came straight down and opened empty.

No.

Even now she still wanted to trust him.

Even now, as she stepped in and pressed the button and took the elevator up to the seventeenth floor, she tried to tell herself that she was wrong.

She had to be wrong, for the man who had made love to her the night before last would not do this. The man who had brought her to his home could not do this to her.

Or had he brought her to his home so that he could free himself to carry on with his ways here?

As she walked along the plush corridor Leila thought of the nights he had returned smelling of perfume.

Leila walked, wondering what one he was behind, and then she heard the one thing she was dreading—the sound of James's voice and a woman laughing behind a hotel door.

She wanted to kick the door, she wanted to burst in on them and scratch his face, but what was the point?

What would it change?

From the start he had told her he was a playboy. She had fallen in love with a man who had, as it turned out, wanted nothing more than a one-night stand.

Circumstance had forced them together.

Tears would not come, anger would not come—all she felt was weary from a world that denied her love over and over.

She asked his driver to take her home.

'You are loved though,' Leila said to the small life inside her. 'You are so loved and you are so wanted and I am going to do everything I can to ensure that you know it every day that I am with you.'

And she would do it alone.

Leila refused to be with a man who did not truly love her, refused to be like James's parents. Her daughter would have a mother who was a strong woman instead of a martyr. Her daughter would have a mother who refused to turn the other cheek.

Anger was coming now and Leila threw a few clothes into the small case she had brought with her from home.

She wanted nothing from him.

Nothing.

Leila tore off the robe he had made for her and put on the one she owned and decided that she would send for her things later. She simply couldn't bear to be here anymore, amongst his things, his scent, close to the man who had stolen her heart.

She took her cash she had saved from working and her passport and put them in her bag and then Leila removed the ring that James had given her at that appalling showy proposal where he had attempted to trap her.

He never would.

I hope she was worth it... Leila texted, and sent it, and then she threw the phone he had given her onto the bed and left the building.

James received the text just as he was getting into his car after leaving The Chatsfield and he immediately called her but it went straight to messages.

'Was Leila okay when you took her home?' James asked his driver.

'She didn't say much,' he answered, 'although she never does.' Then he told James he had taken her to The Chatsfield earlier, and James felt his stomach clench. 'Then I brought her home again.'

He told his driver to wait for him, but as soon as he stepped in their home James knew that she had gone.

Her phone was there, her ring was there, everything was there—just not Leila.

He went to the drawer where she kept all her cash and passport and even without opening it he knew they'd be gone.

He asked his driver to take him to The Harrington and when they told him about their confidentiality policy, one look at his murderous expression and they reneged. 'We haven't had anyone by that name check in.'

'By any other name?' James said, and perhaps it was more his anguish than anger that produced a small shake of the receptionist's head.

James called Manu and told her what had happened and asked her to park herself in The Harrington's reception just in case Leila did arrive.

'I will explain what happened to her if she arrives,' Manu offered, and James thanked her.

She wouldn't go there though, James knew it. Leila would surely know that it would be the first place he would look.

It was the worst evening that turned into the worst night ever.

His driver drove around for hours as James's eyes scanned the busy streets but all to no avail. They went to the Middle Eastern restaurant where she had worked, but no, they hadn't seen her either though they promised to let him know if she did show up.

James rang Spencer and asked him to be on the lookout.

He went to JFK airport where she had stood tasting snow on the night she had arrived here and he actually didn't know what to do.

He had her phone and he even considered

calling her parents, and asking them if he could be put through to Zayn, but James knew the pointlessness of that.

It had finally happened, James thought, when, like some drunk, he found himself calling out her name in the alley where Zayn and he had fought.

She'd made his wish come true because here he was at rock bottom and it looked as if he had lost them both.

Leila could well be on her way back to the cold of her family, to live a life of shame for the street bastard she had produced, and he thought then how her family would be with his daughter.

James looked up at the sky that might be carrying them both away now and there were no stars tonight. There would be no more stars without Leila, but then, as easily as that, he knew where she was.

He found her just a ten-minute walk from his door.

'You shouldn't be here at night on your own,' James said, and he sat on a bench beside her. She could not bring herself to look at him so she looked at the park that she loved where she had for a little while believed she'd belonged.

'The only thing that scares me about this night is that I'll believe your lies and your excuses...' She turned very briefly and it hurt too much to look at his cheating face so she turned away. 'I see you've gone off blonde women since you met me,' Leila sneered in disgust.

'Yep.'

'Well, was she worth it?'

'Actually, no,' James said, and he caught the hand that came to meet him. 'It was Manu...'

'I don't need her name,' Leila said, and she crumpled because even in their darkest row he sat patiently beside her.

'She's been trying to help me so that I can contact your brother, so I can ask him to speak with your family.'

'In a hotel room?' Leila challenged. 'I heard you talking. I heard you laughing...'

'In a business suite,' James said. 'Manu's sitting parked at The Harrington in case you go there.'

'You come home stinking of perfume...

you are laughing with another woman behind closed doors…'

'She was laughing *at* me, Leila,' James said, and something in his voice made her turn around and she watched as he gritted his teeth and then made himself say it.

He took a breath, forced the words out.

'Ana ata'allam al arabiyya.'

She didn't laugh as he told her that he had been learning Arabic. She just stared and did *not* feel a fool for believing him.

'You've been doing that for me?'

'I was hoping that I might be able to speak with your father. I didn't want to tell you because honestly, at times, Leila, I'm not sure if I am ever going to be able to speak it well enough. I didn't want you to get your hopes up and I didn't want you laughing at my attempts.'

'Why would I laugh when I think that is the nicest thing you could do for me. You *are* disappointed it's a girl though…'

'I am beside myself with happiness that we're having a girl,' James said, and his voice had her again believing him. She felt his hand on her stomach, caressing her the way she had wanted him to at the scan. 'I thought I'd lost you both. I thought you were on your way home…'

'I would never keep you from your baby, James,' Leila said, and he nodded as she finally excised that dread forever.

'I've messed up, Leila. Manu was furious about the photo and told me off for touching you in public. She says it will offend not just your family but you. You were right—she wasn't worth it. I should have spoken to you.'

'You should have, for your touch has never offended me,' Leila said. 'Well, once, and I think you registered my displeasure.'

'I did.'

'You haven't made things worse with my family, James. It was terrible already,' Leila said, and started to cry again. He saw the pain and agony and he knew he hadn't caused all of it.

'Maybe they're grieving…' James attempted, because he knew the school of thought about not criticising another's family, but then Leila told him there was more.

'I'm too ashamed to tell you.'

'Never be ashamed with me,' James said.

'She's never loved me…' And he didn't

pat her on the shoulder and say of course she did. He just listened in silent horror as he found out that Leila's mother wouldn't even touch her. 'The maids fed me,' Leila said. 'She hated me so much that she could not bring herself to give me her milk. Even the maids thought me greedy. The night I left she finally told me that she wished it had been me who had died instead of Jasmine. When I called she asked if you said you loved me before or while I parted my legs...'

'I said that I loved you here, Leila.' James pointed out. 'I would never look you in the eye and say that I loved you if I didn't.'

'You would marry me, though, without loving me.'

'I don't know that now,' James admitted. 'I didn't like what I saw at my parents' home. Forcing anyone into anything is not the type of person I usually am. I overreacted when I found out you were pregnant. I was terrified that you'd go back to them.'

'Never,' Leila said. 'She has told me that the palace is better off without me. That the maids are happier now. She says that my father has taken up walking again in the evening...'

'*I'd* take up walking if I was married to that lunatic,' James said. 'I'd be walking morning, noon and night and playing golf too, if I was married to her.'

'You think he does it to get away from her?' Leila frowned.

'Hello!' James said. 'I'll bet the maids aren't as happy as Muriel,' James nudged, and now she properly smiled.

'She's a wicked queen,' James said. 'A wicked, wicked queen. And when our daughter is born *I'm* going to read the fairy tales. You never have to hear her voice or see her ever again unless you choose to.'

'Promise?'

'I promise,' James said. 'And I don't make promises that I might not be able to keep.'

'I believe you.'

He understood now why it had been so impossible for her to believe in his love.

She simply hadn't known what it was.

He kissed her right there in the park and there could have been twenty photographers around them, snapping away—neither cared, neither would notice.

Leila felt his arms wrap around her and the feel of his lips on hers and the caress of his hands on her head and back. His touch was for her.

Love more than existed, it was hers.

James hated Farrah.

More than Leila would ever know. James learned to speak her language and he sat with Manu for hours, working out best how to work through the latest problem that had arisen.

It was early August and their baby was due in two days' time and still James had not been able to marry her. Despite polite letters, despite Manu and Zayn's best attempts, they were blocked at each turn as they tried to get the necessary documentation.

'I'm just going to ask her father,' James said, and then he picked up the phone and spoke in Arabic, not with Farrah but with the king.

He kept it brief.

'I need Leila's birth certificate,' James said, and he knew the drama that would be going on in the palace tonight because he had had the audacity to call. 'If I am to marry her.'

He was met with silence.

'If it isn't here within a week, then I will call every day,' James said. 'Or I will write letters, or I shall email, or I shall write to your press. I hope the noise I make—' Manu's lips pursed because of course what James would do would cause offence, but James had been practising this on his own and he cleared his throat '—will not upset your wife too much and in turn cause too many problems for you?'

It came in the post a week later.

Two days after that he stood with Leila in Central Park and married her on the very spot that James had told her he was *in* love with her. Then they had a photo taken on the bench where Leila had used to sit, drinking coffee, and where he had found her sitting that night. Already they had so many memories.

It was the tiniest of weddings.

Leila wore a cream robe that was threaded with silks that were the colours of the changing trees around them and, as James had said it would be, her favourite place in the world was spectacular at this time of the year.

James wore a suit but not socks and though

he had had his hair cut for the day, on Leila's instructions he hadn't shaved.

They just grabbed passing joggers who were happy to stand for the brief service that was so terribly important to them but especially to Leila, for she wanted to be married before the baby was born.

James had been on the wagon for a little longer than he'd expected to be and tomorrow Leila was being induced because the baby was overdue. It lay low in her belly and kicked its applause as they shared a kiss that some passerby would make a fortune with when they sold it to the press.

No, Spencer would not be pleased.

Care factor?

Zero.

They ate at her favourite restaurant and Habib made sure they had the very best table, but even with the best food and happiness on tap, Leila could not get comfortable.

'Anything?'

'Nothing,' Leila said. 'It's been the best wedding I could have hoped for but now I just want to go home.'

When they got there Esther and Matthew were coming through the foyer and for once not arguing. 'Esther! Matthew!' James called out to them. 'I'd like you meet my wife.'

The pride in James's voice was unmistakable.

'How wonderful!'

It was.

Leila felt completely at home and James never thought he'd be carrying his bride, let alone his very heavily pregnant bride, through any door, but it had never felt more right.

They made love as they had rather frantically for the last week because Muriel had said that it might bring the birth on.

Again, it didn't.

Leila lay afterwards, listening to James sleep and watching the moon drift past her window and thinking of her new name.

Mrs Leila Chatsfield.

It was everything she could have hoped to be.

Her back was hurting and Leila had a long shower, then got back into bed, but nothing, not even happiness, could get her to sleep tonight. As she started to realise what was happening, she let out a moan because this wasn't uncomfortable—this hurt.

'It's a dream,' James said, and he rolled into her. 'It's just a dream.'

'No, James it really hurts…'

'I know…' James started, but then he felt her stomach hard beneath his hand and he understood that it wasn't some nightmare that Leila was locked in.

This was real.

'This isn't pain,' Leila said later at the hospital as she refused an epidural.

Pain was what others did to others.

This was physical.

The need to bear down.

The need to have her husband's face beside hers telling her she was almost there but the knowledge she could do this too.

'A girl,' James said as if they didn't know that already.

And she looked at her baby that lay on her stomach. Even though she may not have been ready for a photo shoot, with her shrivelled skin from being ten days late, she was the most beautiful girl either had seen. Her feet were blue but already turning pink as Leila examined them as well as her once-perfect round nose, which was now flat from the delivery.

Leila watched James's shaking hand cut the cord.

Pink now, she was already searching for food and Leila did not think that her child was greedy as she brought her to her breast.

For a brief moment she wanted to call her mother and share the happy news and she told James the same thing.

'I'm scared she might say something to spoil it.'

'I'll call her if you want,' James said.

'I don't know,' Leila said, and she looked at her tiny defenceless baby. Two minutes after James had done the same to their infant, Leila shook her head and finally *she* cut the last piece of that cord.

She was beautiful, James thought as he looked at Leila sleeping.

They were beautiful, he amended as he looked down at his daughter.

A black-haired mother and a black-haired baby, both of whom had owned James's heart from the moment their eyes had met.

As Leila slept he stood holding his baby and could not believe that she was here or even imagine a world without her anymore.

She was wrapped in a little blanket and had on a hat, but James had taken it off so that he could see her curls. He examined her little nose, which Catherine had explained was a bit squashed from the delivery but would soon be fine.

Excuse me! he thought to himself.

Her nose looked better than perfect to James.

He loved how her fingers closed around his and he thought of all the ski slopes he had hurled himself down with barely a thought and his very reckless ways should surely have him drenched in horror. But when he watched her little fingers close around his, James knew that they had led him to this, to a place where he got to properly feel.

He looked at the flowers that had started to arrive and loathed most of them.

James, unlike Leila, read cards.

Why was there a question mark immersed in exclamation marks in some of their congratulation cards? Why was the rest of the world holding their breath for James to mess up the best thing that had ever happened in his life?

Inexplicable was the love that had walked into The Harrington all those months ago and he no longer needed to explain or excuse that night to others.

Their baby didn't have a name yet and James hoped to God that Leila didn't still want to name her Jasmine.

'You're a good girl,' James said to his daughter, who opened blue eyes to him.

And Leila smiled as she woke, for she knew what he was thinking. Leila had seen the face he had pulled when she'd suggested naming her Jasmine. And she smiled, too, that on the day she had been born he told their baby how good she was, how loved she was.

He made Leila feel like that every day too.

'Can I hold her?' Leila asked.

'Nope, you've had enough goes,' James said. 'It's my turn. You go back to sleep.' Leila smiled as he carried on talking. 'I've managed to put my parents off till tomorrow,' James said. 'Your brother and Sophie are coming in tonight, and they both can't wait to meet her.'

Brother and sister were speaking again.

James had spoken with Zayn and had found out that yes, there was a very good reason that Sophie had revealed James's name to the press and gently he had told Leila why.

Bloody Jasmine, James thought, *making her mischief from the grave.*

He handed Leila their baby and he watched as Leila gazed upon her with so much love and he saw, too, the flicker of confusion, for she had once been that small.

'Are you sure that you don't want me to let your parents know? I don't mind,' James offered—he was the gatekeeper to her heart and would not let her be hurt again. 'I can practise my Arabic,' James said as he cleared the back of his throat, and Leila laughed, but with affection.

'No.' Her moment of weakness just after the birth had long since faded. 'I don't want them near her, ever. I will not let them poison her. They can read it in the press if they choose to, or Zayn can tell them. Really, James, I don't care if they know or if they don't. I have my family and that is you and her.'

She loved him so much and she was not scared to love him now.

Their love was real, it existed, and he showed her that each day.

'We need a name,' James said.

'I've already chosen it.'

'Well, that's the sort of thing that might merit a discussion,' James hastily said, and sat on the bed. 'It's for both parents to decide.'

'Please let me have the name I want for her, James. It would mean so much to me and you know that I would have chosen it after careful thought.'

James took a deep breath and looked at Leila, who had just given him the greatest gift of his life, and really, how could he say no to her for something she really wanted? 'Sure.' He looked at his daughter and was determined to smile and say, 'How beautiful, how perfect,' when Leila said she wanted the baby to be called Jasmine...

'Aqiba,' Leila said.

'Aqiba?' James repeated, and she watched as a very real smile spread across his lips as he worked out the translation.

'Consequence,' Leila said.

No, James thought, a night, such as the one they had shared, could not be without consequence.

James looked at his daughter and said her name. 'Aqiba.'

Their very beautiful consequence.

* * * * *

If you enjoyed this book, look out for the next instalment of THE CHATSFIELD: *VIRGIN'S SWEET REBELLION by Kate Hewitt Coming next month.*

LARGER-PRINT BOOKS!
GET 2 FREE LARGER-PRINT NOVELS PLUS
2 FREE GIFTS!

❧HARLEQUIN®

Romance

From the Heart, For the Heart

YES! Please send me 2 FREE LARGER-PRINT Harlequin® Romance novels and my 2 FREE gifts (gifts are worth about $10). After receiving them, if I don't wish to receive any more books, I can return the shipping statement marked "cancel." If I don't cancel, I will receive 4 brand-new novels every month and be billed just $4.84 per book in the U.S. or $5.24 per book in Canada. That's a savings of at least 19% off the cover price! It's quite a bargain! Shipping and handling is just 50¢ per book in the U.S. and 75¢ per book in Canada.* I understand that accepting the 2 free books and gifts places me under no obligation to buy anything. I can always return a shipment and cancel at any time. Even if I never buy another book, the two free books and gifts are mine to keep forever.

119/319 HDN F43Y

Name	(PLEASE PRINT)

Address		Apt. #

City	State/Prov.	Zip/Postal Code

Signature (if under 18, a parent or guardian must sign)

Mail to the Harlequin® Reader Service:
IN U.S.A.: P.O. Box 1867, Buffalo, NY 14240-1867
IN CANADA: P.O. Box 609, Fort Erie, Ontario L2A 5X3

Want to try two free books from another line?
Call 1-800-873-8635 or visit www.ReaderService.com.

* Terms and prices subject to change without notice. Prices do not include applicable taxes. Sales tax applicable in N.Y. Canadian residents will be charged applicable taxes. Offer not valid in Quebec. This offer is limited to one order per household. Not valid for current subscribers to Harlequin Romance Larger-Print books. All orders subject to credit approval. Credit or debit balances in a customer's account(s) may be offset by any other outstanding balance owed by or to the customer. Please allow 4 to 6 weeks for delivery. Offer available while quantities last.

Your Privacy—The Harlequin® Reader Service is committed to protecting your privacy. Our Privacy Policy is available online at www.ReaderService.com or upon request from the Harlequin Reader Service.

We make a portion of our mailing list available to reputable third parties that offer products we believe may interest you. If you prefer that we not exchange your name with third parties, or if you wish to clarify or modify your communication preferences, please visit us at www.ReaderService.com/consumerchoice or write to us at Harlequin Reader Service Preference Service, P.O. Box 9062, Buffalo, NY 14269. Include your complete name and address.

HRLP13R

ReaderService.com

Manage your account online!

- Review your order history
- Manage your payments
- Update your address

*We've designed
the Harlequin® Reader Service
website just for you.*

Enjoy all the features!

- Reader excerpts from any series
- Respond to mailings and
  special monthly offers
- Discover new series available to you
- Browse the Bonus Bucks catalog
- Share your feedback

Visit us at:
ReaderService.com